MACABRE STORIES

MACABRE STORIES

STORIES

H. P. LOVECRAFT

ARCTURUS

ARCTURUS

This edition published in 2019 by Arcturus Publishing Limited
26/27 Bickels Yard, 151–153 Bermondsey Street,
London SE1 3HA

ISBN: 978-1-78428-828-0
AD005726US

Printed in China

Contents

Introduction

Howard Philips Lovecraft was the pioneer of modern horror fiction. Born in Rhode Island in 1890, his childhood was a troubling one. When he was just three years old, his father was placed in the psychiatric department at Butler Hospital. As a child, Howard was often ill and did not attend school regularly until he was eight years old. But this did not prevent Lovecraft from developing a voracious reading habit.

The death of his grandfather in 1904 profoundly affected Lovecraft. His family fell into poverty, and four years later he suffered a nervous breakdown that prevented him from obtaining his high school diploma. As a young adult, Lovecraft took on an isolated existence, living with his mother and turning his attention to writing. In 1916, he published his first story, 'The Alchemist' in the *United Amateur Press Association*, but this brought him no income. He had to wait until 1922 before he received commercial remuneration for his work. For the next decade, he wrote prolifically. Despite his admiration for Edgar Allan Poe, Lovecraft broke away from earlier traditions of Gothic horror to create something entirely new – the primal gods and the eldritch powers of the mythology of Cthulhu.

During his own lifetime, Lovecraft was virtually unknown, forced to publish his stories in the humble pulp magazines of the era, such as *Weird Tales*. He lived in poverty and his imaginative genius would only be recognized by a later generation.

The selection in *Macabre Stories* represents the beginnings of Lovecraft's career as a horror writer. They follow the period up to the early 1920s when he was still developing his own style. These stories range from fantasy stories inspired by Lord Dunsany to riffs on the Gothic horror genre of the day and demonstrate how the young man developed into the iconic horror writer he became.

Lovecraft's influence on the horror genre has been immense. His writing made possible the careers of writers such as Stephen King, Clive Barker, Neil Gaiman and China Miéville. The Cthulhu Mythos he began was continued by a series of writers and several of his stories have been adapted into films, radio productions and videogames.

THE TOMB

"Sedibus ut saltem placidis in morte quiescam."
—*Virgil*

In relating the circumstances which have led to my confinement within this refuge for the demented, I am aware that my present position will create a natural doubt of the authenticity of my narrative. It is an unfortunate fact that the bulk of humanity is too limited in its mental vision to weigh with patience and intelligence those isolated phenomena, seen and felt only by a psychologically sensitive few, which lie outside its common experience. Men of broader intellect know that there is no sharp distinction betwixt the real and the unreal; that all things appear as they do only by virtue of the delicate individual physical and mental media through which we are made conscious of them; but the prosaic materialism of the majority condemns as madness the flashes of super-sight which penetrate the common veil of obvious empiricism.

My name is Jervas Dudley, and from earliest childhood I have been a dreamer and a visionary. Wealthy beyond the necessity of a commercial life, and temperamentally unfitted for the formal studies and social recreations of my acquaintances, I have dwelt ever in realms apart from the visible world; spending my youth and adolescence in ancient and little-known books, and in roaming the fields and groves of the region near my ancestral home. I do not think that what I read in these books or saw in these fields and groves was exactly what other boys read and saw there; but of this I must say little, since detailed speech would but confirm those cruel slanders upon my intellect which I sometimes overhear from the whispers of the stealthy attendants around me. It is sufficient for me to relate events without analyzing causes.

I have said that I dwelt apart from the visible world, but I have not said that I dwelt alone. This no human creature may do; for lacking the fellowship of the living, he inevitably draws upon the companionship of things that are not, or are no longer, living. Close by my home there lies a singular wooded hollow, in whose twilight deeps I spent most of my time; reading, thinking, and dreaming. Down its moss-covered slopes my first steps of infancy were taken, and around its grotesquely gnarled oak trees my first fancies of boyhood were woven. Well did I come to know the presiding dryads of those trees, and often have I watched their wild dances in the struggling beams of a waning moon – but of these things I must not now speak. I will tell only of the lone tomb in the darkest of the hillside thickets; the deserted tomb of the Hydes, an old and exalted family whose last direct descendant had been laid within its black recesses many decades before my birth.

The vault to which I refer is of ancient granite, weathered and discolored by the mists and dampness of generations. Excavated back into the hillside, the structure is visible only at the entrance. The door, a ponderous and forbidding slab of stone, hangs upon rusted iron hinges, and is fastened *ajar* in a queerly sinister way by means of heavy iron chains and padlocks, according to a gruesome fashion of half a century ago. The abode of the race whose scions are here inurned had once crowned the declivity which holds the tomb, but had long since fallen victim to the flames which sprang up from a disastrous stroke of lightning. Of the midnight storm which destroyed this gloomy mansion, the older inhabitants of the region sometimes speak in hushed and uneasy voices; alluding to what they call "divine wrath" in a manner that in later years vaguely increased the always strong fascination which I felt for the forest-darkened sepulcher. One man only had perished in the fire. When the last of the Hydes was buried in this place of shade and stillness, the sad urnful of ashes had come from a distant land; to which the family had repaired when the mansion burned down. No one remains to lay flowers before the granite portal, and few care to brave the depressing shadows which seem to linger strangely about the water-worn stones.

I shall never forget the afternoon when first I stumbled upon the half-hidden house of death. It was in mid-summer, when the alchemy of Nature transmutes the sylvan landscape to one vivid and almost homogeneous mass of green; when the senses are well-nigh intoxicated with the surging seas of moist verdure and the subtly indefinable odors of the soil and the vegetation. In such surroundings the mind loses its perspective; time and space become trivial and unreal, and echoes of a forgotten prehistoric past beat insistently upon the enthralled consciousness. All day I had been wandering through the mystic groves of the hollow; thinking thoughts I need not discuss, and conversing with things I need not name. In years a child of ten, I had seen and heard many wonders unknown to the throng; and was oddly aged in certain respects. When, upon forcing my way between two savage clumps of briers, I suddenly encountered the entrance of the vault, I had no knowledge of what I had discovered. The dark blocks of granite, the door so curiously ajar, and the funereal carvings above the arch, aroused in me no associations of mournful or terrible character. Of graves and tombs I knew and imagined much, but had on account of my peculiar temperament been kept from all personal contact with churchyards and cemeteries. The strange stone house on the woodland slope was to me only a source of interest and speculation; and its cold, damp interior, into which I vainly peered through the aperture so tantalizingly left, contained for me no hint of death or decay. But in that instant of curiosity was born the madly unreasoning desire which has brought me to this hell of confinement. Spurred on by a voice which must have come from the hideous soul of the forest, I resolved to enter the beckoning gloom in spite of the ponderous chains which barred my passage. In the waning light of day I alternately rattled the rusty impediments with a view to throwing wide the stone door, and essayed to squeeze my slight form through the space already provided; but neither plan met with success. At first curious, I was now frantic; and when in the thickening twilight I returned to my home, I had sworn to the hundred gods of the grove that *at any cost* I would some day force an entrance to the black, chilly depths that seemed calling out to me. The physician with the iron-gray beard who comes each day to my room once told a visitor that this decision marked the beginning of a pitiful monomania; but I will leave final judgment to my readers when they shall have learnt all.

The months following my discovery were spent in futile attempts to force the complicated padlock of the slightly open vault, and in carefully guarded inquiries regarding the nature and history of the structure. With the traditionally receptive ears of the small boy, I learned much; though an habitual secretiveness caused me to tell no one of my information or my resolve. It is perhaps worth mentioning that I was not at all surprised or terrified on learning of the nature of the vault. My rather original ideas regarding life and death had caused me to associate the cold clay with the breathing body in a vague fashion; and I felt that the great and sinister family of the burned-down mansion was in some way represented within the stone space I sought to explore. Mumbled tales of the weird rites and godless revels of bygone years in the ancient hall gave to me a new and potent interest in the tomb, before whose door I would sit for hours at a time each day. Once I thrust a candle within the nearly closed entrance, but could see nothing save a flight of damp stone steps leading downward. The odor of the place repelled yet bewitched me. I felt I had known it before, in a past remote beyond all recollection; beyond even my tenancy of the body I now possess.

The year after I first beheld the tomb, I stumbled upon a worm-eaten translation of Plutarch's *Lives* in the book-filled attic of my home. Reading the life of Theseus, I was much impressed by that passage telling of the great stone beneath which the boyish hero was to find his tokens of destiny whenever he should become old enough to lift its enormous weight. This legend had the effect of dispelling my keenest impatience to enter the vault, for it made me feel that the time was not yet ripe. Later, I told myself, I should grow to a strength and ingenuity which might enable me to unfasten the heavily chained door with ease; but until then I would do better by conforming to what seemed the will of Fate.

Accordingly my watches by the dank portal became less persistent, and much of my time was spent in other though equally strange pursuits. I would sometimes rise very quietly in the night, stealing out to walk in those churchyards and places of burial from which I had been kept by my parents. What I did there I may not say, for I am not now sure of the reality of certain things; but I know that on the day after such a nocturnal ramble I would often astonish those about me with my knowledge of topics almost forgotten for many generations. It was after a night like this that I shocked the community with a queer conceit about the burial of the rich and celebrated Squire Brewster, a maker of local history who was interred in 1711, and whose slate headstone, bearing a graven skull and crossbones, was slowly crumbling to powder. In a moment of childish imagination I vowed not only that the undertaker, Goodman Simpson, had stolen the silver-buckled shoes, silken hose, and satin small-clothes of the deceased before burial; but that the Squire himself, not fully inanimate, had turned twice in his mound-covered coffin on the day after interment.

But the idea of entering the tomb never left my thoughts; being indeed stimulated by the unexpected genealogical discovery that my own maternal ancestry possessed at least a slight link with the supposedly extinct family of the Hydes. Last of my paternal race, I was likewise the last of this older and more mysterious line. I began to feel that the tomb was *mine,* and to look forward with hot eagerness to the time when I might pass within that stone door and down those slimy stone steps in the dark. I now formed the habit of *listening* very intently at the slightly open portal, choosing my favorite hours of midnight stillness for the odd vigil. By the time I came of age, I had made a small clearing in the thicket before the mold-stained facade of the hillside, allowing the surrounding vegetation to encircle and overhang the space like the walls and roof of a sylvan bower. This bower was my temple, the fastened door my shrine, and here I would lie outstretched on the mossy ground, thinking strange thoughts and dreaming strange dreams.

The night of the first revelation was a sultry one. I must have fallen asleep from fatigue, for it was with a distinct sense of awakening that I heard the *voices*. Of those tones and accents I hesitate to speak; of their *quality* I will not speak; but I may say that they presented certain uncanny differences in vocabulary, pronunciation, and mode of utterance. Every shade of New England dialect, from the uncouth syllables of the Puritan colonists to the precise rhetoric of fifty years ago, seemed represented in that shadowy colloquy, though it was only later that I noticed the fact. At the time, indeed, my attention was distracted from this matter by another phenomenon; a phenomenon so fleeting that I could not take oath upon its reality. I barely fancied that as I awoke, a *light* had been hurriedly extinguished within the sunken sepulcher. I do not think I was either astounded or panic-stricken, but I know that I was greatly and permanently *changed* that night. Upon returning home I went with much directness to a rotting chest in the attic, wherein I found the key which next day unlocked with ease the barrier I had so long stormed in vain.

It was in the soft glow of late afternoon that I first entered the vault on the abandoned slope. A spell was upon me, and my heart leaped with an exultation I can but ill describe. As I closed the door behind me and descended the dripping steps by the light of my lone candle, I seemed to know the way; and though the candle sputtered with the stifling reek of the place, I felt singularly at home in the musty, charnel-house air. Looking about me, I beheld many marble slabs bearing coffins, or the remains of coffins. Some of these were sealed and intact, but others had nearly vanished, leaving the silver handles and plates isolated amidst certain curious heaps of whitish dust. Upon one plate I read the name of Sir Geoffrey Hyde, who had come from Sussex in 1640 and died here a few years later. In a conspicuous alcove was one fairly well-preserved and untenanted casket, adorned with a single name which brought to me both a smile and a shudder. An odd impulse caused me to climb upon the broad slab, extinguish my candle, and lie down within the vacant box.

In the gray light of dawn I staggered from the vault and locked the chain of the door behind me. I was no longer a young man, though but twenty-one winters had chilled my bodily frame. Early-rising villagers who observed my homeward progress looked at me strangely, and marveled at the signs of ribald revelry which they saw in one whose life was known to be sober and solitary. I did not appear before my parents till after a long and refreshing sleep.

Henceforward I haunted the tomb each night; seeing, hearing, and doing things I must never reveal. My speech, always susceptible to environmental influences, was the first thing to succumb to the change; and my suddenly acquired archaism of diction was soon remarked upon. Later a queer boldness and recklessness came into my demeanor, till I unconsciously grew to possess the bearing of a man of the world despite my lifelong seclusion. My formerly silent tongue waxed voluble with the easy grace of a Chesterfield or the godless cynicism of a Rochester. I displayed a peculiar erudition utterly unlike the fantastic, monkish lore over which I had pored in youth; and covered the flyleaves of my books with facile impromptu epigrams which brought up suggestions of Gay, Prior, and the sprightliest of the Augustan wits and rimesters. One morning at breakfast I came close to disaster by declaiming in palpably liquorish accents an effusion of eighteenth-century Bacchanalian mirth; a bit of Georgian playfulness never recorded in a book, which ran something like this:

Come hither, my lads, with your tankards of ale,
And drink to the present before it shall fail;
Pile each on your platter a mountain of beef,
For 'tis eating and drinking that bring us relief:
    So fill up your glass,
    For life will soon pass;
When you're dead ye'll ne'er drink to your king or
your lass!

Anacreon had a red nose, so they say;
But what's a red nose if ye're happy and gay?
Gad split me! I'd rather be red whilst I'm here,
Than white as a lily – and dead half a year!
    So Betty, my miss,
    Come give me a kiss;
In hell there's no innkeeper's daughter like this!

Young Harry, propp'd up just as straight as he's able,
Will soon lose his wig and slip under the table;
But fill up your goblets and pass 'em around—
Better under the table than under the ground!
    So revel and chaff
    As ye thirstily quaff:
Under sixs feet of dirt 'tis less easy to laugh!

The fiend strike me blue! I'm scarce able to walk,
And damn me if I can stand upright or talk!
Here, landlord, bid Betty to summon a chair;
I'll try home for a while, for my wife is not there!
    So lend me a hand;
    I'm not able to stand,
But I'm gay whilst I linger on top of the land!

About this time I conceived my present fear of fire and thunder-
storms. Previously indifferent to such things, I had now an

unspeakable horror of them; and would retire to the innermost recesses of the house whenever the heavens threatened an electrical display. A favorite haunt of mine during the day was the ruined cellar of the mansion that had burned down, and in fancy I would picture the structure as it had been in its prime. On one occasion I startled a villager by leading him confidently to a shallow sub-cellar, of whose existence I seemed to know in spite of the fact that it had been unseen and forgotten for many generations.

At last came that which I had long feared. My parents, alarmed at the altered manner and appearance of their only son, commenced to exert over my movements a kindly espionage which threatened to result in disaster. I had told no one of my visits to the tomb, having guarded my secret purpose with religious zeal since childhood; but now I was forced to exercise care in threading the mazes of the wooded hollow, that I might throw off a possible pursuer. My key to the vault I kept suspended from a cord about my neck, its presence known only to me. I never carried out of the sepulcher any of the things I came upon whilst within its walls.

One morning as I emerged from the damp tomb and fastened the chain of the portal with none too steady hand, I beheld in an adjacent thicket the dreaded face of a watcher. Surely the end was near; for my bower was discovered, and the objective of my nocturnal journeys revealed. The man did not accost me, so I hastened home in an effort to overhear what he might report to my careworn father. Were my sojourns beyond the chained door about to be proclaimed to the world? Imagine my delighted astonishment on hearing the spy inform my parent in a cautious whisper *that I had spent the night in the bower outside the tomb*; my sleep-filmed eyes fixed upon the crevice where the padlocked portal stood ajar! By what miracle had the watcher been thus deluded? I was now convinced that a supernatural agency protected me. Made bold by this heaven-sent circumstance, I began to resume perfect openness in going to the vault;

confident that no one could witness my entrance. For a week I tasted to the full the joys of that charnel conviviality which I must not describe, when the *thing* happened, and I was borne away to this accursed abode of sorrow and monotony.

I should not have ventured out that night; for the taint of thunder was in the clouds, and a hellish phosphorescence rose from the rank swamp at the bottom of the hollow. The call of the dead, too, was different. Instead of the hillside tomb, it was the charred cellar on the crest of the slope whose presiding daemon beckoned to me with unseen fingers. As I emerged from an intervening grove upon the plain before the ruin, I beheld in the misty moonlight a thing I had always vaguely expected. The mansion, gone for a century, once more reared its stately height to the raptured vision; every window ablaze with the splendor of many candles. Up the long drive rolled the coaches of the Boston gentry, whilst on foot came a numerous assemblage of powdered exquisites from the neighboring mansions. With this throng I mingled, though I knew I belonged with the hosts rather than with the guests. Inside the hall were music, laughter, and wine on every hand. Several faces I recognized; though I should have known them better had they been shriveled or eaten away by death and decomposition. Amidst a wild and reckless throng I was the wildest and most abandoned. Gay blasphemy poured in torrents from my lips, and in my shocking sallies I heeded no law of God, Man, or Nature. Suddenly a peal of thunder, resonant even above the din of the swinish revelry, clave the very roof and laid a hush of fear upon the boisterous company. Red tongues of flame and searing gusts of heat engulfed the house; and the roysterers, struck with terror at the descent of a calamity which seemed to transcend the bounds of unguided Nature, fled shrieking into the night. I alone remained, riveted to my seat by a groveling fear which I had never felt before. And then a second horror took possession of my soul. Burned alive to ashes, my body dispersed by the four winds, *I might never lie in the tomb of the Hydes!* Was not my coffin prepared for me? Had I not a

right to rest till eternity amongst the descendants of Sir Geoffrey
Hyde? Aye! I would claim my heritage of death, even though my
soul go seeking through the ages for another corporeal tenement
to represent it on that vacant slab in the alcove of the vault.
Jervas Hyde should never share the sad fate of Palinurus!

As the phantom of the burning house faded, I found myself
screaming and struggling madly in the arms of two men, one of
whom was the spy who had followed me to the tomb. Rain was
pouring down in torrents, and upon the southern horizon were
flashes of the lightning that had so lately passed over our heads.
My father, his face lined with sorrow, stood by as I shouted my
demands to be laid within the tomb; frequently admonishing my
captors to treat me as gently as they could. A blackened circle
on the floor of the ruined cellar told of a violent stroke from
the heavens; and from this spot a group of curious villagers with
lanterns were prying a small box of antique workmanship which
the thunderbolt had brought to light. Ceasing my futile and now
objectless writhing, I watched the spectators as they viewed the
treasure-trove, and was permitted to share in their discoveries.
The box, whose fastenings were broken by the stroke which
had unearthed it, contained many papers and objects of value;
but I had eyes for one thing alone. It was the porcelain miniature of a young man in a smartly curled bag-wig, and bore the
initials "J. H." The face was such that as I gazed, I might well
have been studying my mirror.

On the following day I was brought to this room with the
barred windows, but I have been kept informed of certain things
through an aged and simple-minded servitor, for whom I bore a
fondness in infancy, and who like me loves the churchyard. What
I have dared relate of my experiences within the vault has brought
me only pitying smiles. My father, who visits me frequently,
declares that at no time did I pass the chained portal, and swears
that the rusted padlock had not been touched for fifty years
when he examined it. He even says that all the village knew of
my journeys to the tomb, and that I was often watched as I slept

in the bower outside the grim facade, my half-open eyes fixed on the crevice that leads to the interior. Against these assertions I have no tangible proof to offer, since my key to the padlock was lost in the struggle on that night of horrors. The strange things of the past which I learnt during those nocturnal meetings with the dead he dismisses as the fruits of my lifelong and omnivorous browsing amongst the ancient volumes of the family library. Had it not been for my old servant Hiram, I should have by this time become quite convinced of my madness.

But Hiram, loyal to the last, has held faith in me, and has done that which impels me to make public at least a part of my story. A week ago he burst open the lock which chains the door of the tomb perpetually ajar, and descended with a lantern into the murky depths. On a slab in an alcove he found an old but empty coffin whose tarnished plate bears the single word *"Jervas."* In that coffin and in that vault they have promised me I shall be buried.

DAGON

I am writing this under an appreciable mental strain, since by
tonight I shall be no more. Penniless, and at the end of my
supply of the drug which alone makes life endurable, I can bear
the torture no longer; and shall cast myself from this garret
window into the squalid street below. Do not think from my
slavery to morphine that I am a weakling or a degenerate. When
you have read these hastily scrawled pages you may guess,
though never fully realize, why it is that I must have forgetfulness
or death.

It was in one of the most open and least frequented parts of
the broad Pacific that the packet of which I was supercargo fell
a victim to the German sea-raider. The great war was then at its
very beginning, and the ocean forces of the Hun had not
completely sunk to their later degradation; so that our vessel
was made a legitimate prize, whilst we of her crew were treated
with all the fairness and consideration due us as naval prisoners.
So liberal, indeed, was the discipline of our captors, that five days
after we were taken I managed to escape alone in a small boat
with water and provisions for a good length of time.

When I finally found myself adrift and free, I had but little
idea of my surroundings. Never a competent navigator, I could
only guess vaguely by the sun and stars that I was somewhat
south of the equator. Of the longitude I knew nothing, and no
island or coastline was in sight. The weather kept fair, and for
uncounted days I drifted aimlessly beneath the scorching sun;
waiting either for some passing ship, or to be cast on the shores
of some habitable land. But neither ship nor land appeared, and
I began to despair in my solitude upon the heaving vastnesses
of unbroken blue.

The change happened whilst I slept. Its details I shall never
know; for my slumber, though troubled and dream-infested,

was continuous. When at last I awaked, it was to discover myself half sucked into a slimy expanse of hellish black mire which extended about me in monotonous undulations as far as I could see, and in which my boat lay grounded some distance away.

Though one might well imagine that my first sensation would be of wonder at so prodigious and unexpected a transformation of scenery, I was in reality more horrified than astonished; for there was in the air and in the rotting soil a sinister quality which chilled me to the very core. The region was putrid with the carcasses of decaying fish, and of other less describable things which I saw protruding from the nasty mud of the unending plain. Perhaps I should not hope to convey in mere words the unutterable hideousness that can dwell in absolute silence and barren immensity. There was nothing within hearing, and nothing in sight save a vast reach of black slime; yet the very complete-ness of the stillness and the homogeneity of the landscape oppressed me with a nauseating fear.

The sun was blazing down from a sky which seemed to me almost black in its cloudless cruelty; as though reflecting the inky marsh beneath my feet. As I crawled into the stranded boat I realized that only one theory could explain my position. Through some unprecedented volcanic upheaval, a portion of the ocean floor must have been thrown to the surface, exposing regions which for innumerable millions of years had lain hidden under unfathomable watery depths. So great was the extent of the new land which had risen beneath me, that I could not detect the faintest noise of the surging ocean, strain my ears as I might. Nor were there any sea-fowl to prey upon the dead things.

For several hours I sat thinking or brooding in the boat, which lay upon its side and afforded a slight shade as the sun moved across the heavens. As the day progressed, the ground lost some of its stickiness, and seemed likely to dry sufficiently for traveling purposes in a short time. That night I slept but little, and the next day I made for myself a pack containing food and water, preparatory to an overland journey in search of the vanished sea and possible rescue.

On the third morning I found the soil dry enough to walk upon with ease. The odor of the fish was maddening; but I was too much concerned with graver things to mind so slight an evil, and set out boldly for an unknown goal. All day I forged steadily westward, guided by a far-away hummock which rose higher than any other elevation on the rolling desert. That night I encamped, and on the following day still traveled toward the hummock, though that object seemed scarcely nearer than when I had first espied it. By the fourth evening I attained the base of the mound, which turned out to be much higher than it had appeared from a distance; an intervening valley setting it out in sharper relief from the general surface. Too weary to ascend, I slept in the shadow of the hill.

I know not why my dreams were so wild that night; but ere the waning and fantastically gibbous moon had risen far above the eastern plain, I was awake in a cold perspiration, determined to sleep no more. Such visions as I had experienced were too much for me to endure again. And in the glow of the moon I saw how unwise I had been to travel by day. Without the glare of the parching sun, my journey would have cost me less energy; indeed, I now felt quite able to perform the ascent which had deterred me at sunset. Picking up my pack, I started for the crest of the eminence.

I have said that the unbroken monotony of the rolling plain was a source of vague horror to me; but I think my horror was greater when I gained the summit of the mound and looked down the other side into an immeasurable pit or canyon, whose black recesses the moon had not yet soared high enough to illumine. I felt myself on the edge of the world; peering over the rim into a fathomless chaos of eternal night. Through my terror ran curious reminiscences of *Paradise Lost,* and of Satan's hideous climb through the unfashioned realms of darkness.

As the moon climbed higher in the sky, I began to see that the slopes of the valley were not quite so perpendicular as I had imagined. Ledges and outcroppings of rock afforded fairly easy foot-holds for a descent, whilst after a drop of a few hundred feet, the declivity became very gradual. Urged on by an impulse which I cannot definitely analyze, I scrambled with difficulty down the rocks and stood on the gentler slope beneath, gazing into the Stygian deeps where no light had yet penetrated.

All at once my attention was captured by a vast and singular object on the opposite slope, which rose steeply about an hundred yards ahead of me; an object that gleamed whitely in the newly bestowed rays of the ascending moon. That it was merely a gigantic piece of stone, I soon assured myself; but I was conscious of a distinct impression that its contour and position were not altogether the work of Nature. A closer scrutiny filled me with sensations I cannot express; for despite its enormous magnitude, and its position in an abyss which had yawned at the bottom of the sea since the world was young, I perceived beyond a doubt that the strange object was a well-shaped monolith whose massive bulk had known the workmanship and perhaps the worship of living and thinking creatures.

Dazed and frightened, yet not without a certain thrill of the scientist's or archeologist's delight, I examined my surroundings more closely. The moon, now near the zenith, shone weirdly and vividly above the towering steeps that hemmed in the chasm, and revealed the fact that a far-flung body of water flowed at the bottom, winding out of sight in both directions, and almost lapping my feet as I stood on the slope. Across the chasm, the wavelets washed the base of the Cyclopean monolith; on whose surface I could now trace both inscriptions and crude sculptures. The writing was in a system of hieroglyphics unknown to me, and unlike anything I had ever seen in books; consisting for the most part of conventionalized aquatic symbols such as fishes, eels, octopi, crustaceans, mollusks, whales, and the like. Several characters obviously represented marine things which are unknown to the modern world, but whose decomposing forms I had observed on the ocean-risen plain.

It was the pictorial carving, however, that did most to hold me spellbound. Plainly visible across the intervening water on account of their enormous size, were an array of bas-reliefs whose subjects would have excited the envy of a Doré. I think that these things were supposed to depict men – at least, a certain sort of men; though the creatures were shewn disporting like fishes in the waters of some marine grotto, or paying homage at some monolithic shrine which appeared to be under the waves as well. Of their faces and forms I dare not speak in detail; for the mere remembrance makes me grow faint. Grotesque beyond the imagination of a Poe or a Bulwer, they were damnably human in general outline despite webbed hands and feet, shockingly wide and flabby lips, glassy, bulging eyes, and other features less pleasant to recall. Curiously enough, they seemed to have been chiseled badly out of proportion with their scenic background; for one of the creatures was shewn in the act of killing a whale represented as but little larger than himself. I remarked, as I say, their grotesqueness and strange size; but in a moment decided that they were merely the imaginary gods of some primitive fishing or seafaring tribe; some tribe whose last descendant had perished eras before the first ancestor of the Piltdown or Neanderthal Man was born. Awestruck at this unexpected glimpse into a past beyond the conception of the most daring anthropologist, I stood musing whilst the moon cast queer reflections on the silent channel before me.

Then suddenly I saw it. With only a slight churning to mark its rise to the surface, the thing slid into view above the dark waters. Vast, Polyphemus-like, and loathsome, it darted like a stupendous monster of nightmares to the monolith, about which it flung its gigantic scaly arms, the while it bowed its hideous head and gave vent to certain measured sounds. I think I went mad then.

Of my frantic ascent of the slope and cliff, and of my delirious journey back to the stranded boat, I remember little. I believe I sang a great deal, and laughed oddly when I was unable to sing. I have indistinct recollections of a great storm some time after I reached the boat; at any rate, I know that I heard peals of thunder and other tones which Nature utters only in her wildest moods.

When I came out of the shadows I was in a San Francisco hospital; brought thither by the captain of the American ship which had picked up my boat in mid-ocean. In my delirium I had said much, but found that my words had been given scant attention. Of any land upheaval in the Pacific, my rescuers knew nothing; nor did I deem it necessary to insist upon a thing which I knew they could not believe. Once I sought out a celebrated ethnologist, and amused him with peculiar questions regarding the ancient Philistine legend of Dagon, the Fish-God; but soon perceiving that he was hopelessly conventional, I did not press my inquiries.

It is at night, especially when the moon is gibbous and waning, that I see the thing. I tried morphine; but the drug has given only transient surcease, and has drawn me into its clutches as a hopeless slave. So now I am to end it all, having written a full account for the information or the contemptuous amusement of my fellow men. Often I ask myself if it could not all have been a pure phantasm – a mere freak of fever as I lay sun-stricken and raving in the open boat after my escape from the German man-of-war. This I ask myself, but ever does there come before me a hideously vivid vision in reply. I cannot think of the deep sea without shuddering at the nameless things that may at this very moment be crawling and floundering on its slimy bed, worshiping their ancient stone idols and carving their own detestable likenesses on submarine obelisks of water-soaked granite. I dream of a day when they may rise above the billows to drag down in their reeking talons the remnants of puny, war-exhausted mankind – of a day when the land shall sink, and the dark ocean floor shall ascend amidst universal pandemonium.

The end is near. I hear a noise at the door, as of some immense slippery body lumbering against it. It shall not find me. God, *that hand!* The window! The window!

A REMINISCENCE OF
DR. SAMUEL JOHNSON

The Privilege of Reminiscence, however rambling or tiresome, is one generally allow'd to the very aged; indeed, 'tis frequently by means of such Recollections that the obscure occurrences of History, and the lesser Anecdotes of the Great, are transmitted to Posterity.

Tho' many of my readers have at times observ'd and remark'd a Sort of antique Flow in my Stile of Writing, it hath pleased me to pass amongst the Members of this Generation as a young Man, giving out the Fiction that I was born in 1890, in *America.* I am now, however, resolv'd to unburthen myself of a Secret which I have hitherto kept thro' Dread of Incredulity; and to impart to the Publick a true knowledge of my long years, in order to gratifie their taste for authentick Information of an Age with whose famous Personages I was on familiar Terms. Be it then known that I was born on the family Estate in *Devonshire,* of the 10th day of August, 1690 (or in the new *Gregorian* Stile of Reckoning, the 20th of August), being therefore now in my 228th year. Coming early to *London,* I saw as a Child many of the celebrated Men of King *William's* Reign, including the lamented Mr. *Dryden,* who sat much at the Tables of *Will's* Coffee-House. With Mr. *Addison* and Dr. *Swift* I later became very well acquainted, and was an even more familiar Friend to Mr. *Pope,* whom I knew and respected till the Day of his Death. But since it is of my more recent Associate, the late Dr. *Johnson,* that I am at this time desir'd to write; I will pass over my Youth for the present.

I had first Knowledge of the Doctor in May of the year 1738, tho' I did not at that Time meet him. Mr. *Pope* had just compleated his Epilogue to his *Satires* (the Piece beginning: "Not twice a Twelvemonth you appear in Print."), and had arrang'd for its

Publication. On the very Day it appear'd, there was also publish'd a Satire in Imitation of *Juvenal,* intitul'd "*London,*" by the then unknown *Johnson;* and this so struck the Town, that many Gentlemen of Taste declared, it was the Work of a greater Poet than Mr. *Pope.* Notwithstanding what some Detractors have said of Mr. *Pope's* petty Jealousy, he gave the Verses of his new Rival no small Praise; and having learnt thro' Mr. *Richardson* who the Poet was, told me "that Mr. *Johnson* wou'd soon be *deterré.*"

I had no personal Acquaintance with the Doctor till 1763, when I was presented to him at the *Mitre* Tavern by Mr. *James Boswell,* a young *Scotchman* of excellent Family and great Learning, but small Wit, whose metrical Effusions I had sometimes revis'd.

Dr. *Johnson,* as I beheld him, was a full, pursy Man, very ill drest, and of slovenly Aspect. I recall him to have worn a bushy Bob-Wig, untyed and without Powder, and much too small for his Head. His cloaths were of rusty brown, much wrinkled, and with more than one Button missing. His Face, too full to be handsom, was likewise marred by the Effects of some scrofulous Disorder; and his Head was continually rolling about in a sort of convulsive way. Of this Infirmity, indeed, I had known before; having heard of it from Mr. *Pope,* who took the Trouble to make particular Inquiries.

Being nearly seventy-three, full nineteen Years older than Dr. *Johnson* (I say Doctor, tho' his Degree came not till two Years afterward), I naturally expected him to have some Regard for my Age; and was therefore not in that Fear of him, which others confess'd. On my asking him what he thought of my favourable Notice of his Dictionary in *The Londoner,* my periodical Paper, he said: "Sir, I possess no Recollection of having perus'd your Paper, and have not a great Interest in the Opinions of the less thoughtful Part of Mankind." Being more than a little piqued at the Incivility of one whose Celebrity made me solicitous of his Approbation, I ventur'd to retaliate in kind, and told him, I was surpris'd that a Man of Sense shou'd judge the Thoughtfulness of one whose Productions he admitted never having read. "Why, Sir," reply'd *Johnson,* "I do not require to become familiar with a Man's Writings in order to estimate the Superficiality of his Attainments, when he plainly shews it by his Eagerness to mention his own Productions in the first Question he puts to me." Having thus become Friends, we convers'd on many Matters. When, to agree with him, I said I was distrustful of the Authenticity of *Ossian's* Poems, Mr. *Johnson* said: "That, Sir, does not do your Understanding particular Credit; for what all the Town is sensible of, is no great Discovery for a *Grub-Street* Critick to make. You might as well say, you have a strong Suspicion that *Milton* wrote *Paradise Lost*!"

I thereafter saw *Johnson* very frequently, most often at Meetings of THE LITERARY CLUB, which was founded the next Year by the Doctor, together with Mr. *Burke,* the parliamentary Orator, Mr. *Beauclerk,* a Gentleman of Fashion, Mr. *Langton,* a pious Man and Captain of Militia, Sir J. *Reynolds,* the widely known Painter, Dr. *Goldsmith,* the prose and poetick Writer, Dr. *Nugent,* father-in-law to Mr. *Burke,* Sir *John Hawkins,* Mr. *Anthony Chamier,* and my self. We assembled generally at seven o'clock of an Evening, once a Week, at the *Turk's-Head,* in *Gerrard-Street, Soho,* till that Tavern was sold and made into a private Dwelling; after which Event we mov'd our Gatherings successively to *Prince's* in *Sackville-Street, Le Tellier's* in *Dover-Street,* and *Parsloe's* and *The Thatched House* in *St. James's-Street.* In these Meetings we preserv'd a remarkable Degree of Amity and Tranquillity, which contrasts very favourably with some of the Dissensions and Disruptions I observe in the literary and amateur Press Associations of today. This Tranquillity was the more remarkable, because we had amongst us Gentlemen of very opposed Opinions. Dr. *Johnson* and I, as well as many others, were high Tories; whilst Mr. *Burke* was a *Whig,* and against the *American* War, many of his Speeches on that Subject having been widely publish'd. The least congenial Member was one of the Founders, Sir *John Hawkins,* who hath since written many misrepresentations of our Society. Sir *John,* an eccentrick Fellow, once declin'd to pay his part of the Reckoning for Supper, because 'twas his Custom at Home to eat no Supper. Later he insulted Mr. *Burke* in so intolerable a Manner, that we all took Pains to shew our Disapproval; after which Incident he came no more to our Meetings. However, he never openly fell out with the Doctor, and was the Executor of his Will; tho' Mr. *Boswell* and others have Reason to question the genuineness of his Attachment. Other and later Members of the CLUB were Mr. *David Garrick,* the Actor and early Friend of Dr. *Johnson,* Messieurs *Tho.* and *Jos. Warton,* Dr. *Adam Smith,* Dr. *Percy,* Author of the "Reliques," Mr. *Edw. Gibbon,* the Historian, Dr. *Burney,* the Musician, Mr. *Malone,* the Critick, and Mr. *Boswell.* Mr. *Garrick* obtain'd Admittance only with Difficulty; for the Doctor, notwithstanding his great Friendship, was for ever affecting to decry the Stage and all Things connected with it. *Johnson,* indeed, had a most singular Habit of speaking for *Davy* when others were against him, and of arguing against him, when others were for him. I have no Doubt but that he sincerely lov'd Mr. *Garrick,* for he never alluded to him as he did to *Foote,* who was a very coarse Fellow despite his comick Genius. Mr. *Gibbon* was none too well lik'd, for he had an odious sneering Way which offended even those of us who most admir'd his historical Productions. Mr. *Goldsmith,* a little Man very vain of his Dress and very deficient in Brilliancy of Conversation, was my particular Favourite; since I was equally unable to shine in the Discourse. He was vastly jealous of Dr. *Johnson,* tho' none the less liking and respecting him. I remember that once a Foreigner, a *German,* I think, was in our Company; and that whilst *Goldsmith* was speaking, he observ'd the Doctor preparing to utter something. Unconsciously looking upon *Goldsmith* as a meer Encumbrance when compar'd to the greater Man, the Foreigner bluntly interrupted him and incurr'd his lasting Hostility by crying, "Hush, Toctor *Shonson* iss going to speak!"

In this luminous Company I was tolerated more because of

my Years than for my Wit or Learning; being no Match at all for the rest. My Friendship for the celebrated Monsieur *Voltaire* was ever a Cause of Annoyance to the Doctor; who was deeply orthodox, and who us'd to say of the *French* Philosopher: "Vir est acerrimi Ingenii et paucarum Literarum."

Mr. *Boswell,* a little teazing Fellow whom I had known for some Time previously, us'd to make Sport of my aukward Manners and old-fashion'd Wig and Cloaths. Once coming in a little the worse for Wine (to which he was addicted) he endeavour'd to lampoon me by means of an Impromptu in verse, writ on the Surface of the Table; but lacking the Aid he usually had in his Composition, he made a bad grammatical Blunder. I told him, he shou'd not try to pasquinade the Source of his Poesy. At another Time *Bozzy* (as we us'd to call him) complain'd of my Harshness toward new Writers in the Articles I prepar'd for *The Monthly Review.* He said, I push'd every Aspirant off the Slopes of Parnassus. "Sir," I reply'd, "you are mistaken. They who lose their Hold do so from their own Want of Strength; but desiring to conceal their Weakness, they attribute the Absence of Success to the first Critick that mentions them." I am glad to recall that Dr. *Johnson* upheld me in this Matter.

Dr. *Johnson* was second to no Man in the Pains he took to revise the bad Verses of others; indeed, 'tis said that in the book of poor blind old Mrs. Williams, there are scarce two lines which are not the Doctor's. At one Time *Johnson* recited to me some lines by a Servant to the Duke of *Leeds,* which had so amus'd him, that he had got them by Heart. They are on the Duke's Wedding, and so much resemble in Quality the Work of other and more recent poetick Dunces, that I cannot forbear copying them:

> When the Duke of Leeds shall marry'd be
> To a fine young Lady of high Quality
> How happy will that Gentlewoman be
> In his Grace of Leeds' good Company.

I ask'd the Doctor, if he had ever try'd making Sense of this Piece; and upon his saying he had not, I amus'd myself with the following Amendment of it:

> When Gallant LEEDS auspiciously shall wed
>> The virtuous Fair, of antient Lineage bred,
> How must the Maid rejoice with conscious Pride
>> To win so great an Husband to her Side!

On shewing this to Dr. *Johnson,* he said, "Sir, you have straightened out the Feet, but you have put neither Wit nor Poetry into the Lines."

It wou'd afford me Gratification to tell more of my Experiences with Dr. *Johnson* and his circle of Wits; but I am an old Man, and easily fatigued. I seem to ramble along without much Logick or Continuity when I endeavour to recall the Past; and fear I light upon but few Incidents which others have not before discuss'd. Shou'd my present Recollections meet with Favour, I might later set down some further Anecdotes of old Times of which I am the only Survivor. I recall many things of *Sam Johnson* and his Club, having kept up my Membership in the Latter long after the Doctor's Death, at which I sincerely mourn'd. I remember how *John Burgoyne,* Esq., the General, whose Dramatick and Poetical Works were printed after his Death, was blackballed by three Votes; probably because of his unfortunate Defeat in the *American* War, at *Saratoga.* Poor *John!* His Son fared better, I think, and was made a Baronet. But I am very tired. I am old, very old, and it is Time for my Afternoon Nap.

SWEET ERMENGARDE
OR, THE HEART OF
A COUNTRY GIRL

Chapter I
A SIMPLE RUSTIC MAID

Ermengarde Stubbs was the beauteous blonde daughter of Hiram Stubbs, a poor but honest farmer-bootlegger of Hogton, Vt. Her name was originally Ethyl Ermengarde, but her father persuaded her to drop the praenomen after the passage of the 18th Amendment, averring that it made him thirsty by reminding him of ethyl alcohol, C_2H_5OH. His own products contained mostly methyl or wood alcohol, CH_3OH. Ermengarde confessed to sixteen summers, and branded as mendacious all reports to the effect that she was thirty. She had large black eyes, a prominent Roman nose, light hair which was never dark at the roots except when the local drug store was short on supplies, and a beautiful but inexpensive complexion. She was about 5ft 5.33in tall, weighed 115.47lb. on her father's copy scales - also off them - and was adjudged most lovely by all the village swains who admired her father's farm and liked his liquid crops.

Ermengarde's hand was sought in matrimony by two ardent lovers. 'Squire Hardman, who had a mortgage on the old home, was very rich and elderly. He was dark and cruelly handsome, and always rode horseback and carried a riding-crop. Long had he sought the radiant Ermengarde, and now his ardor was fanned to fever heat by a secret known to him alone - for upon the humble acres of Farmer Stubbs he had discovered a vein of rich GOLD!! "Aha!" said he, "I will win the maiden ere her parent knows of his unsuspected wealth, and join to my fortune a greater fortune still!" And so he began to call twice a week instead of once as before.

But alas for the sinister designs of a villain – 'Squire Hardman was not the only suitor for the fair one. Close by the village dwelt another – the handsome Jack Manly, whose curly yellow hair had won the sweet Ermengarde's affection when both were toddling youngsters at the village school. Jack had long been too bashful to declare his passion, but one day while strolling along a shady lane by the old mill with Ermengarde, he had found courage to utter that which was within his heart.

"O light of my life," said he, "my soul is so overburdened that I must speak! Ermengarde, my ideal [he pronounced it i-deel!], life has become an empty thing without you. Beloved of my spirit, behold a suppliant kneeling in the dust before thee. Ermengarde – oh, Ermengarde, raise me to an heaven of joy and say that you will some day be mine! It is true that I am poor, but have I not youth and strength to fight my way to fame? This I can do only for you, dear Ethyl – pardon me, Ermengarde – my only, my most precious—" but here he paused to wipe his eyes and mop his brow, and the fair responded:

"Jack – my angel – at last – I mean, this is so unexpected and quite unprecedented! I had never dreamed that you entertained sentiments of affection in connexion with one so lowly as Farmer Stubbs' child – for I am still but a child! Such is your natural nobility that I had feared – I mean thought – you would be blind to such slight charms as I possess, and that you would seek your fortune in the great city; there meeting and wedding one of those more comely damsels whose splendor we observe in fashion books.

"But, Jack, since it is really I whom you adore, let us waive all needless circumlocution. Jack – my darling – my heart has long been susceptible to your manly graces. I cherish an affection for thee – consider me thine own and be sure to buy the ring at Perkins' hardware store where they have such nice imitation diamonds in the window."

"Ermengarde, me love!"

"Jack - my precious!"

"My darling!"

"My own!"

"My Gawd!"

Chapter II
AND THE VILLAIN STILL PURSUED HER

But these tender passages, sacred though their fervor, did not pass unobserved by profane eyes; for crouched in the bushes and gritting his teeth was the dastardly 'Squire Hardman! When the lovers had finally strolled away he leapt out into the lane, viciously twirling his moustache and riding-crop, and kicking an unquestionably innocent cat who was also out strolling.

"Curses!" he cried - Hardman, not the cat - "I am foiled in my plot to get the farm and the girl! But Jack Manly shall never succeed! I am a man of power - and we shall see!"

Thereupon he repaired to the humble Stubbs' cottage, where he found the fond father in the still-cellar washing bottles under the supervision of the gentle wife and mother, Hannah Stubbs. Coming directly to the point, the villain spoke:

"Farmer Stubbs, I cherish a tender affection of long standing for your lovely offspring, Ethyl Ermengarde. I am consumed with love, and wish her hand in matrimony. Always a man of few words, I will not descend to euphemism. Give me the girl or I will foreclose the mortgage and take the old home!"

"But, Sir," pleaded the distracted Stubbs while his stricken spouse merely glowered, "I am sure the child's affections are elsewhere placed."

"She must be mine!" sternly snapped the sinister 'squire. "I will make her love me - none shall resist my will! Either she becomes muh wife or the old homestead goes!"

And with a sneer and flick of his riding-crop 'Squire Hardman strode out into the night.

Scarce had he departed, when there entered by the back door the radiant lovers, eager to tell the senior Stubbses of their new-found happiness. Imagine the universal consternation which reigned when all was known! Tears flowed like white ale, till suddenly Jack remembered he was the hero and raised his head, declaiming in appropriately virile accents:

"Never shall the fair Ermengarde be offered up to this beast as a sacrifice while I live! I shall protect her - she is mine, mine, mine - and then some! Fear not, dear father and mother to be - I will defend you all! You shall have the old home still [adverb, not noun - although Jack was by no means out of sympathy with Stubbs' kind of farm produce] and I shall lead to the altar the beauteous Ermengarde, loveliest of her sex! To perdition with the crool 'squire and his ill-gotten gold - the right shall always win, and a hero is always in the right! I will go to the great city and there make a fortune to save you all ere the mortgage fall due! Farewell, my love - I leave you now in tears, but I shall return to pay off the mortgage and claim you as my bride!"

"Jack, my protector!"

"Ermie, my sweet roll!"

"Dearest!"

"Darling! - and don't forget that ring at Perkins'."

"Oh!"

"Ah!"

Chapter III

A DASTARDLY ACT

But the resourceful 'Squire Hardman was not so easily to be foiled. Close by the village lay a disreputable settlement of unkempt shacks, populated by a shiftless scum who lived by

thieving and other odd jobs. Here the devilish villain secured
two accomplices – ill-favored fellows who were very clearly no
gentlemen. And in the night the evil three broke into the Stubbs
cottage and abducted the fair Ermengarde, taking her to a
wretched hovel in the settlement and placing her under the
charge of Mother Maria, a hideous old hag. Farmer Stubbs was
quite distracted, and would have advertised in the papers if the
cost had been less than a cent a word for each insertion.
Ermengarde was firm, and never wavered in her refusal to wed
the villain.

"Aha, my proud beauty," quoth he, "I have ye in me power,
and sooner or later I will break that will of thine! Meanwhile
think of your poor old father and mother as turned out of hearth
and home and wandering helpless through the meadows!"

"Oh, spare them, spare them!" said the maiden.

"Neverr . . . ha ha ha ha!" leered the brute.

And so the cruel days sped on, while all in ignorance young
Jack Manly was seeking fame and fortune in the great city.

Chapter IV
SUBTLE VILLAINY

One day as 'Squire Hardman sat in the front parlor of his
expensive and palatial home, indulging in his favorite pastime
of gnashing his teeth and swishing his riding-crop, a great thought
came to him; and he cursed aloud at the statue of Satan on the
onyx mantelpiece.

"Fool that I am!" he cried. "Why did I ever waste all this
trouble on the girl when I can get the farm by simply foreclosing? I never thought of that! I will let the girl go, take the
farm, and be free to wed some fair city maid like the leading
lady of that burlesque troupe which played last week at the
Town Hall!"

And so he went down to the settlement, apologized to

Ermengarde, let her go home, and went home himself to plot new crimes and invent new modes of villainy.

The days wore on, and the Stubbses grew very sad over the coming loss of their home and still but nobody seemed able to do anything about it. One day a party of hunters from the city chanced to stray over the old farm, and one of them found the gold!! Hiding his discovery from his companions, he feigned rattlesnake-bite and went to the Stubbs' cottage for aid of the usual kind. Ermengarde opened the door and saw him. He also saw her, and in that moment resolved to win her and the gold. "For my old mother's sake I must" – he cried loudly to himself. "No sacrifice is too great!"

Chapter V
THE CITY CHAP

Algernon Reginald Jones was a polished man of the world from the great city, and in his sophisticated hands our poor little Ermengarde was as a mere child. One could almost believe that sixteen-year-old stuff. Algy was a fast worker, but never crude. He could have taught Hardman a thing or two about finesse in sheiking. Thus only a week after his advent to the Stubbs family circle, where he lurked like the vile serpent that he was, he had persuaded the heroine to elope! It was in the night that she went leaving a note for her parents, sniffing the familiar mash for the last time, and kissing the cat goodbye – touching stuff! On the train Algernon became sleepy and slumped down in his seat, allowing a paper to fall out of his pocket by accident. Ermengarde, taking advantage of her supposed position as a bride-elect, picked up the folded sheet and read its perfumed expanse – when lo! she almost fainted! It was a love letter from another woman!!

"Perfidious deceiver!" she whispered at the sleeping Algernon, "so this is all that your boasted fidelity amounts to! I am done with you for all eternity!"

So saying, she pushed him out the window and settled down for a much needed rest.

Chapter VI
ALONE IN THE GREAT CITY

When the noisy train pulled into the dark station at the city, poor helpless Ermengarde was all alone without the money to get back to Hogton. "Oh why," she sighed in innocent regret, "didn't I take his pocket-book before I pushed him out? Oh well, I should worry! He told me all about the city so I can easily earn enough to get home if not to pay off the mortgage!"

But alas for our little heroine – work is not easy for a green-horn to secure, so for a week she was forced to sleep on park benches and obtain food from the bread-line. Once a wily and wicked person, perceiving her helplessness, offered her a position as dish-washer in a fashionable and depraved cabaret; but our heroine was true to her rustic ideals and refused to work in such a gilded and glittering palace of frivolity – especially since she was offered only $3.00 per week with meals but no board. She tried to look up Jack Manly, her one-time lover, but he was nowhere to be found. Perchance, too, he would not have known her; for in her poverty she had perforce become a brunette again, and Jack had not beheld her in that state since school days. One day she found a neat but costly purse in the park; and after seeing that there was not much in it, took it to the rich lady whose card proclaimed her ownership. Delighted beyond words at the honesty of this forlorn waif, the aristocratic Mrs. Van Itty adopted Ermengarde to replace the little one who had been stolen from her so many years ago. "How like my precious Maude," she sighed, as she watched the fair brunette return to blondeness. And so several weeks passed, with the old folks at home tearing their hair and the wicked 'Squire Hardman chuckling devilishly.

Chapter VII
HAPPY EVER AFTERWARD

One day the wealthy heiress Ermengarde S. Van Itty hired a new second assistant chauffeur. Struck by something familiar in his face, she looked again and gasped. Lo! it was none other than the perfidious Algernon Reginald Jones, whom she had pushed from a car window on that fateful day! He had survived – this much was almost immediately evident. Also, he had wed the other woman, who had run away with the milkman and all the money in the house. Now wholly humbled, he asked forgiveness of our heroine, and confided to her the whole tale of the gold on her father's farm. Moved beyond words, she raised his salary a dollar a month and resolved to gratify at last that always unquenchable anxiety to relieve the worry of the old folks. So one bright day Ermengarde motored back to Hogton and arrived at the farm just as 'Squire Hardman was foreclosing the mortgage and ordering the old folks out.

"Stay, villain!" she cried, flashing a colossal roll of bills. "You are foiled at last! Here is your money – now go, and never darken our humble door again!"

Then followed a joyous reunion, whilst the 'squire twisted his moustache and riding-crop in bafflement and dismay. But hark! What is this? Footsteps sound on the old gravel walk, and who should appear but our hero, Jack Manly – worn and seedy, but radiant of face. Seeking at once the downcast villain, he said:

"'Squire – lend me a ten-spot, will you? I have just come back from the city with my beauteous bride, the fair Bridget Goldstein, and need something to start things on the old farm." Then turning to the Stubbses, he apologized for his inability to pay off the mortgage as agreed.

"Don't mention it," said Ermengarde, "prosperity has come to us, and I will consider it sufficient payment if you will forget forever the foolish fancies of our childhood."

All this time Mrs. Van Itty had been sitting in the motor waiting for Ermengarde; but as she lazily eyed the sharp-faced Hannah Stubbs a vague memory started from the back of her brain. Then it all came to her, and she shrieked accusingly at the agrestic matron.

"You – you – Hannah Smith – I know you now! Twenty-eight years ago you were my baby Maude's nurse and stole her from the cradle!! Where, oh, where is my child?" Then a thought came as the lightning in a murky sky. "*Ermengarde* – you say she is *your* daughter. . . . She is mine! Fate has restored to me my old chee-ild – my tiny Maudie! – Ermengarde – Maude – come to your mother's loving arms!!!"

But Ermengarde was doing some tall thinking. How could she get away with the sixteen-year-old stuff if she had been stolen twenty-eight years ago? And if she was not Stubbs' daughter the gold would never be hers. Mrs. Van Itty was rich, but 'Squire Hardman was richer. So, approaching the dejected villain, she inflicted upon him the last terrible punishment.

"'Squire, dear," she murmured, "I have reconsidered all. I love you and your naive strength. Marry me at once or I will have you prosecuted for that kidnapping last year. Foreclose your mortgage and enjoy with me the gold your cleverness discovered. Come, dear!" And the poor dub did.

MEMORY

In the valley of Nis the accursed waning moon shines thinly, tearing a path for its light with feeble horns through the lethal foliage of a great upas-tree. And within the depths of the valley, where the light reaches not, move forms not meet to be beheld. Rank is the herbage on each slope, where evil vines and creeping plants crawl amidst the stones of ruined palaces, twining tightly about broken columns and strange monoliths, and heaving up marble pavements laid by forgotten hands. And in trees that grow gigantic in crumbling courtyards leap little apes, while in and out of deep treasure-vaults writhe poison serpents and scaly things without a name.

Vast are the stones which sleep beneath coverlets of dank moss, and mighty were the walls from which they fell. For all time did their builders erect them, and in sooth they yet serve nobly, for beneath them the gray toad makes his habitation.

At the very bottom of the valley lies the river Than, whose waters are slimy and filled with weeds. From hidden springs it rises, and to subterranean grottoes it flows, so that the Daemon of the Valley knows not why its waters are red, nor whither they are bound.

The Genie that haunts the moonbeams spake to the Daemon of the Valley, saying, "I am old, and forget much. Tell me the deeds and aspect and name of them who built these things of stone." And the Daemon replied, "I am Memory, and am wise in lore of the past, but I too am old. These beings were like the waters of the river Than, not to be understood. Their deeds I recall not, for they were but of the moment. Their aspect I recall dimly, for it was like to that of the little apes in the trees. Their name I recall clearly, for it rhymed with that of the river. These beings of yesterday were called Man."

So the Genie flew back to the thin horned moon, and the Daemon looked intently at a little ape in a tree that grew in a crumbling courtyard.

OLD BUGS

AN EXTEMPORANEOUS SOB STORY
BY MARCUS LOLLIUS, PROCONSUL OF GAUL

Sheehan's Pool Room, which adorns one of the lesser alleys in the heart of Chicago's stockyard district, is not a nice place. Its air, freighted with a thousand odors such as Coleridge may have found at Cologne, too seldom knows the purifying rays of the sun; but fights for space with the acrid fumes of unnumbered cheap cigars and cigarettes which dangle from the coarse lips of unnumbered human animals that haunt the place day and night. But the popularity of Sheehan's remains unimpaired; and for this there is a reason – a reason obvious to anyone who will take the trouble to analyze the mixed stenches prevailing there. Over and above the fumes and sickening closeness rises an aroma once familiar throughout the land, but now happily banished to the back streets of life by the edict of a benevolent government – the aroma of strong, wicked whiskey – a precious kind of forbidden fruit indeed in this year of grace 1950.

Sheehan's is the acknowledged center to Chicago's subterranean traffic in liquor and narcotics, and as such has a certain dignity which extends even to the unkempt attachés of the place; but there was until lately one who lay outside the pale of that dignity – one who shared the squalor and filth, but not the importance, of Sheehan's. He was called "Old Bugs," and was the most disreputable object in a disreputable environment. What he had once been, many tried to guess; for his language and mode of utterance when intoxicated to a certain degree were such as to excite wonderment; but what he *was,* presented less difficulty – for "Old Bugs," in superlative degree, epitomized the pathetic species known as the "bum" or the "down-and-outer." Whence he had come, no one could tell. One night he had burst

wildly into Sheehan's, foaming at the mouth and screaming for
whiskey and hasheesh; and having been supplied in exchange
for a promise to perform odd jobs, had hung about ever since,
mopping floors, cleaning cuspidors and glasses, and attending to
an hundred similar menial duties in exchange for the drink and
drugs which were necessary to keep him alive and sane.

He talked but little, and usually in the common jargon of the
underworld; but occasionally, when inflamed by an unusually
generous dose of crude whiskey, would burst forth into strings
of incomprehensible polysyllables and snatches of sonorous
prose and verse which led certain habitués to conjecture that
he had seen better days. One steady patron – a bank defaulter
under cover – came to converse with him quite regularly, and
from the tone of his discourse ventured the opinion that he had
been a writer or professor in his day. But the only tangible clue
to Old Bugs' past was a faded photograph which he constantly
carried about with him – the photograph of a young woman of
noble and beautiful features.This he would sometimes draw from
his tattered pocket, carefully unwrap from its covering of tissue
paper, and gaze upon for hours with an expression of ineffable
sadness and tenderness. It was not the portrait of one whom an
underworld denizen would be likely to know, but of a lady of
breeding and quality, garbed in the quaint attire of thirty years
before. Old Bugs himself seemed also to belong to the past, for
his nondescript clothing bore every hallmark of antiquity. He
was a man of immense height, probably more than six feet,
though his stooping shoulders sometimes belied this fact. His
hair, a dirty white and falling out in patches, was never combed;
and over his lean face grew a mangy stubble of coarse beard
which seemed always to remain at the bristling stage – never
shaven – yet never long enough to form a respectable set of
whiskers. His features had perhaps been noble once, but were
now seamed with the ghastly effects of terrible dissipation. At
one time – probably in middle life – he had evidently been
grossly fat; but now he was horribly lean, the purple flesh hanging

in loose pouches under his bleary eyes and upon his cheeks. Altogether, Old Bugs was not pleasing to look upon.

The disposition of Old Bugs was as odd as his aspect. Ordinarily he was true to the derelict type – ready to do anything for a nickel or a dose of whiskey or hasheesh – but at rare intervals he shewed the traits which earned him his name. Then he would try to straighten up, and a certain fire would creep into the sunken eyes. His demeanor would assume an unwonted grace and even dignity; and the sodden creatures around him would sense something of superiority – something which made them less ready to give the usual kicks and cuffs to the poor butt and drudge. At these times he would shew a sardonic humor and make remarks which the folk of Sheehan's deemed foolish and irrational. But the spells would soon pass, and once more Old Bugs would resume his eternal floor-scrubbing and cuspidor-cleaning. But for one thing Old Bugs would have been an ideal slave to the establishment – and that one thing was his conduct when young men were introduced for their first drink. The old man would then rise from the floor in anger and excitement, muttering threats and warnings, and seeking to dissuade the novices from embarking upon their course of "seeing life as it is." He would sputter and fume, exploding into sesquipedalian admonitions and strange oaths, and animated by a frightful earnestness which brought a shudder to more than one drug-racked mind in the crowded room. But after a time his alcohol-enfeebled brain would wander from the subject, and with a foolish grin he would turn once more to his mop or cleaning-rag.

I do not think that many of Sheehan's regular patrons will ever forget the day that young Alfred Trever came. He was rather a "find" – a rich and high-spirited youth who would "go the limit" in anything he undertook – at least, that was the verdict of Pete Schultz, Sheehan's "runner," who had come across the boy at Lawrence College, in the small town of Appleton, Wisconsin. Trever was the son of prominent parents in Appleton.

His father, Karl Trever, was an attorney and citizen of distinction, whilst his mother had made an enviable reputation as a poetess under her maiden name of Eleanor Wing. Alfred was himself a scholar and poet of distinction, though cursed with a certain childish irresponsibility which made him an ideal prey for Sheehan's runner. He was blond, handsome, and spoiled; vivacious and eager to taste the several forms of dissipation about which he had read and heard. At Lawrence he had been prominent in the mock-fraternity of "Tappa Tappa Keg," where he was the wildest and merriest of the wild and merry young roysterers; but this immature, collegiate frivolity did not satisfy him. He knew deeper vices through books, and he now longed to know them at first hand. Perhaps this tendency toward wildness had been stimulated somewhat by the repression to which he had been subjected at home; for Mrs. Trever had particular reason for training her only child with rigid severity. She had, in her own youth, been deeply and permanently impressed with the horror of dissipation by the case of one to whom she had for a time been engaged.

Young Galpin, the fiancé in question, had been one of Appleton's most remarkable sons. Attaining distinction as a boy through his wonderful mentality, he won vast fame at the University of Wisconsin, and at the age of twenty-three returned to Appleton to take up a professorship at Lawrence and to slip a diamond upon the finger of Appleton's fairest and most brilliant daughter. For a season all went happily, till without warning the storm burst. Evil habits, dating from a first drink taken years before in woodland seclusion, made themselves manifest in the young professor; and only by a hurried resignation did he escape a nasty prosecution for injury to the habits and morals of the pupils under his charge. His engagement broken, Galpin moved east to begin life anew; but before long, Appletonians heard of his dismissal in disgrace from New York University, where he had obtained an instructorship in English. Galpin now devoted his time to the library and lecture platform, preparing volumes and speeches on various subjects connected with *belles lettres,* and always shewing a genius so remarkable that it seemed as if the public must sometime pardon him for his past mistakes. His impassioned lectures in defense of Villon, Poe, Verlaine, and Oscar Wilde were applied to himself as well, and in the short Indian summer of his glory there was talk of a renewed engagement at a certain cultured home on Park Avenue. But then the blow fell. A final disgrace, compared to which the others had been as nothing, shattered the illusions of those who had come to believe in Galpin's reform; and the young man abandoned his name and disappeared from public view. Rumor now and then associated him with a certain "Consul Hasting" whose work for the stage and for motion-picture companies attracted a certain degree of attention because of its scholarly breadth and depth; but Hasting soon disappeared from the public eye, and Galpin became only a name for parents to quote in warning accents. Eleanor Wing soon celebrated her marriage to Karl Trever, a rising young lawyer, and of her former admirer retained only enough memory to dictate the naming of her only son, and the moral guidance of that handsome and headstrong youth. Now, in spite of all that guidance, Alfred Trever was at Sheehan's and about to take his first drink.

"Boss," cried Schultz, as he entered the vile-smelling room with his young victim, "meet my friend Al Trever, bes' li'l' sport up at Lawrence – thas' 'n Appleton, Wis., y' know. Some swell guy, too – 's father's a big corp'ration lawyer up in his burg, 'n' 's mother's some lit'ry genius. He wants to see life as she is – wants to know what the real lightnin' juice tastes like – so jus' remember he's me friend an' treat 'im right."

As the names Trever, Lawrence, and Appleton fell on the air, the loafers seemed to sense something unusual. Perhaps it was only some sound connected with the clicking balls of the pool tables or the rattling glasses that were brought from the cryptic regions in the rear – perhaps only that, plus some strange rustling of the dirty draperies at the one dingy window – but many thought that someone in the room had gritted his teeth and drawn a very sharp breath.

"Glad to know you, Sheehan," said Trever in a quiet, well-bred tone. "This is my first experience in a place like this, but I am a student of life, and don't want to miss any experience. There's poetry in this sort of thing, you know – or perhaps you don't know, but it's all the same."

"Young feller," responded the proprietor, "ya come tuh th' right place tuh see life. We got all kinds here – reel life an' a good time. The damn' government can try tuh make folks good ef it wants tuh, but it can't stop a feller from hittin' 'er up when he feels like it. Whaddya want, feller – booze, coke, or some other sorta dope? Yuh can't ask for nothin' we ain't got."

Habitués say that it was at this point they noticed a cessation in the regular, monotonous strokes of the mop.

"I want whiskey – good old-fashioned rye!" exclaimed Trever enthusiastically. "I'll tell you, I'm good and tired of water after reading of the merry bouts fellows used to have in the old days. I can't read an Anacreontic without watering at the mouth – and it's something a lot stronger than water that my mouth waters for!"

"Anacreontic – what 'n hell's that?" several hangers-on looked up as the young man went slightly beyond their depth. But the bank defaulter under cover explained to them that Anacreon was a gay old dog who lived many years ago and wrote about the fun he had when all the world was just like Sheehan's.

"Let me see, Trever," continued the defaulter, "didn't Schultz say your mother is a literary person, too?"

"Yes, damn it," replied Trever, "but nothing like the old Teian! She's one of those dull, eternal moralizers that try to take all the joy out of life. Namby-pamby sort – ever heard of her? She writes under her maiden name of Eleanor Wing."

Here it was that Old Bugs dropped his mop.

"Well, here's yer stuff," announced Sheehan jovially as a tray of bottles and glasses was wheeled into the room. "Good old rye, an' as fiery as ya kin find anyw'eres in Chi'."

The youth's eyes glistened and his nostrils curled at the fumes of the brownish fluid which an attendant was pouring out for him. It repelled him horribly, and revolted all his inherited delicacy; but his determination to taste life to the full remained with him, and he maintained a bold front. But before his resolution was put to the test, the unexpected intervened. Old Bugs, springing up from the crouching position in which he had hitherto been, leaped at the youth and dashed from his hands the uplifted glass, almost simultaneously attacking the tray of bottles and glasses with his mop, and scattering the contents upon the floor in a confusion of odoriferous fluid and broken bottles and tumblers. Numbers of men, or things which had been men, dropped to the floor and began lapping at the puddles of spilled liquor, but most remained immovable, watching the unprecedented actions of the barroom drudge and derelict. Old Bugs straightened up before the astonished Trever, and in a mild and cultivated voice said, "Do not do this thing. I was like you once, and I did it. Now I am like – this."

"What do you mean, you damned old fool?" shouted Trever. "What do you mean by interfering with a gentleman in his pleasures?"

Sheehan, now recovering from his astonishment, advanced and laid a heavy hand on the old waif's shoulder.

"This is the last time for you, old bird!" he exclaimed furiously. "When a gen'l'man wants tuh take a drink here, by God, he shall, without you interferin'. Now get th' hell outa here afore I kick hell outa ya."

But Sheehan had reckoned without scientific knowledge of abnormal psychology and the effects of nervous stimulus. Old Bugs, obtaining a firmer hold on his mop, began to wield it like the javelin of a Macedonian hoplite, and soon cleared a considerable space around himself, meanwhile shouting various disconnected bits of quotation, among which was prominently repeated, " . . . the sons of Belial, blown with insolence and wine."

The room became pandemonium, and men screamed and

howled in fright at the sinister being they had aroused. Trever seemed dazed in the confusion, and shrank to the wall as the strife thickened. "He shall not drink! He shall not drink!" Thus roared Old Bugs as he seemed to run out of – or rise above – quotations. Policemen appeared at the door, attracted by the noise, but for a time they made no move to intervene. Trever, now thoroughly terrified and cured forever of his desire to see life via the vice route, edged closer to the blue-coated newcomers. Could he but escape and catch a train for Appleton, he reflected, he would consider his education in dissipation quite complete.

Then suddenly Old Bugs ceased to wield his javelin and stopped still – drawing himself up more erectly than any denizen of the place had ever seen him before. *"Ave, Caesar, moriturus te saluto!"* he shouted, and dropped to the whiskey-reeking floor, never to rise again.

Subsequent impressions will never leave the mind of young Trever. The picture is blurred, but ineradicable. Policemen plowed a way through the crowd, questioning everyone closely both about the incident and about the dead figure on the floor. Sheehan especially did they ply with inquiries, yet without eliciting any information of value concerning Old Bugs. Then the bank defaulter remembered the picture, and suggested that it be viewed and filed for identification at police headquarters. An officer bent reluctantly over the loathsome glassy-eyed form and found the tissue-wrapped cardboard, which he passed around among the others.

"Some chicken!" leered a drunken man as he viewed the beautiful face, but those who were sober did not leer, looking with respect and abashment at the delicate and spiritual features. No one seemed able to place the subject, and all wondered that the drug-degraded derelict should have such a portrait in his possession – that is, all but the bank defaulter, who was mean-while eyeing the intruding bluecoats rather uneasily. *He* had seen a little deeper beneath Old Bugs' mask of utter degradation.

Then the picture was passed to Trever, and a change came

over the youth. After the first start, he replaced the tissue wrapping around the portrait, as if to shield it from the sordidness of the place. Then he gazed long and searchingly at the figure on the floor, noting its great height, and the aristocratic cast of features which seemed to appear now that the wretched flame of life had flickered out. No, he said hastily, as the question was put to him, he did not know the subject of the picture. It was so old, he added, that no one now could be expected to recognize it.

But Alfred Trever did not speak the truth, as many guessed when he offered to take charge of the body and secure its interment in Appleton. Over the library mantel in his home hung the exact replica of that picture, and all his life he had known and loved its original.

For the gentle and noble features were those of his own mother.

THE TRANSITION
OF JUAN ROMERO

Of the events which took place at the Norton Mine on October 18th and 19th, 1894, I have no desire to speak. A sense of duty to science is all that impels me to recall, in these last years of my life, scenes and happenings fraught with a terror doubly acute because I cannot wholly define it. But I believe that before I die I should tell what I know of the – shall I say transition – of Juan Romero.

My name and origin need not be related to posterity; in fact, I fancy it is better that they should not be, for when a man suddenly migrates to the States or the Colonies, he leaves his past behind him. Besides, what I once was is not in the least relevant to my narrative; save perhaps the fact that during my service in India I was more at home amongst white-bearded native teachers than amongst my brother-officers. I had delved not a little into odd Eastern lore when overtaken by the calamities which brought about my new life in America's vast West – a life wherein I found it well to accept a name – my present one – which is very common and carries no meaning.

In the summer and autumn of 1894 I dwelt in the drear expanses of the Cactus Mountains, employed as a common laborer at the celebrated Norton Mine; whose discovery by an aged prospector some years before had turned the surrounding region from a nearly unpeopled waste to a seething cauldron of sordid life. A cavern of gold, lying deep below a mountain lake, had enriched its venerable finder beyond his wildest dreams, and now formed the seat of extensive tunneling operations on the part of the corporation to which it had finally been sold. Additional grottoes had been found, and the yield of yellow metal was exceedingly great; so that a mighty and heterogeneous army of miners toiled day and night in the numerous passages and rock hollows. The Superintendent, a Mr. Arthur, often discussed the singularity of the local geological formations; speculating on the probable extent of the chain of caves, and estimating the future of the titanic mining enterprise. He considered the auriferous cavities the result of the action of water, and believed the last of them would soon be opened.

It was not long after my arrival and employment that Juan Romero came to the Norton Mine. One of a large herd of unkempt Mexicans attracted thither from the neighboring country, he at first commanded attention only because of his features; which though plainly of the Red Indian type, were yet remarkable for their light color and refined conformation, being vastly unlike those of the average "Greaser" or Piute of the locality. It is curious that although he differed so widely from the mass of Hispanicized and tribal Indians, Romero gave not the least impression of Caucasian blood. It was not the Castilian conquistador or the American pioneer, but the ancient and noble Aztec, whom imagination called to view when the silent peon would rise in the early morning and gaze in fascination at the sun as it crept above the eastern hills, meanwhile stretching out his arms to the orb as if in the performance of some rite whose nature he did not himself comprehend. But save for his face, Romero was not in any way suggestive of nobility. Ignorant and dirty, he was at home amongst the other brown-skinned Mexicans; having come (so I was afterward told) from the very lowest sort of surroundings. He had been found as a child in a crude mountain hut, the only survivor of an epidemic which had stalked lethally by. Near the hut, close to a rather unusual rock fissure, had lain two skeletons, newly picked by vultures, and presumably forming the sole remains of his parents. No one recalled their identity, and they were soon forgotten by the many. Indeed, the crumbling of the adobe hut and the closing of the rock fissure by a subsequent avalanche had helped to efface even the scene from recollection. Reared by a Mexican cattle-thief who had given him his name, Juan differed little from his fellows.

The attachment which Romero manifested toward me was undoubtedly commenced through the quaint and ancient Hindoo ring which I wore when not engaged in active labor. Of its nature, and manner of coming into my possession, I cannot speak. It was my last link with a chapter of life forever closed, and I valued it highly. Soon I observed that the odd-looking Mexican was likewise interested; eyeing it with an expression that banished all suspicion of mere covetousness. Its hoary hieroglyphs seemed to stir some faint recollection in his untutored but active mind, though he could not possibly have beheld their like before. Within a few weeks after his advent, Romero was like a faithful servant to me; this notwithstanding the fact that I was myself but an ordinary miner. Our conversation was necessarily limited. He knew but a few words of English, while I found my Oxonian Spanish was something quite different from the patois of the peon of New Spain.

The event which I am about to relate was unheralded by long premonitions. Though the man Romero had interested me, and though my ring had affected him peculiarly, I think that neither of us had any expectation of what was to follow when the great blast was set off. Geological considerations had dictated an extension of the mine directly downward from the deepest part of the subterranean area; and the belief of the Superintendent that only solid rock would be encountered, had led to the placing of a prodigious charge of dynamite. With this work Romero and I were not connected, wherefore our first knowledge of extraordinary conditions came from others. The charge, heavier perhaps than had been estimated, had seemed to shake the entire mountain. Windows in shanties on the slope outside were shattered by the shock, whilst miners throughout the nearer passages were knocked from their feet. Jewel Lake, which lay above the scene of action, heaved as in a tempest. Upon investigation it was seen that a new abyss yawned indefinitely below the seat of the blast; an abyss so monstrous that no handy line might fathom it, nor any lamp illuminate it. Baffled, the excavators sought a conference with the Superintendent, who ordered great lengths of rope to be taken to the pit, and spliced and lowered without cessation till a bottom might be discovered.

Shortly afterward the pale-faced workmen apprized the Superintendent of their failure. Firmly though respectfully they signified their refusal to revisit the chasm, or indeed to work further in the mine until it might be sealed. Something beyond their experience was evidently confronting them, for so far as they could ascertain, the void below was infinite. The Superintendent did not reproach them. Instead, he pondered deeply, and made many plans for the following day. The night shift did not go on that evening.

At two in the morning a lone coyote on the mountain began to howl dismally. From somewhere within the works a dog barked in answer; either to the coyote - or to something else. A storm was gathering around the peaks of the range, and weirdly shaped clouds scudded horribly across the blurred patch of celestial light which marked a gibbous moon's attempts to shine through many layers of cirro-stratus vapors. It was Romero's voice, coming from the bunk above, that awakened me; a voice excited and tense with some vague expectation I could not understand:

"¡Madre de Dios! - el sonido - ese sonido - ¡oiga Vd! ¿lo oye Vd? - Señor, THAT SOUND!"

I listened, wondering what sound he meant. The coyote, the dog, the storm, all were audible; the last named now gaining ascendancy as the wind shrieked more and more frantically. Flashes of lightning were visible through the bunk-house window. I questioned the nervous Mexican, repeating the sounds I had heard:

"¿El coyote? - ¿el perro? - ¿el viento?"

But Romero did not reply. Then he commenced whispering as in awe:

"El ritmo, Señor - el ritmo de la tierra - THAT THROB DOWN IN THE GROUND!"

And now I also heard; heard and shivered and without knowing why. Deep, deep, below me was a sound - a rhythm, just as the peon had said - which, though exceedingly faint, yet dominated even the dog, the coyote, and the increasing tempest. To seek to describe it were useless - for it was such that no description is possible. Perhaps it was like the pulsing of the engines far down in a great liner, as sensed from the deck, yet it was not so mechanical; not so devoid of the element of life and consciousness. Of all its qualities, *remoteness* in the earth most impressed me. To my mind rushed fragments of a passage in Joseph Glanvill which Poe has quoted with tremendous effect -

" - the vastness, profundity, and unsearchableness of His works, *which have a depth in them greater than the well of Democritus.*"

Suddenly Romero leaped from his bunk; pausing before me to gaze at the strange ring on my hand, which glistened queerly in every flash of lightning, and then staring intently in the direction of the mine shaft. I also rose, and both stood motionless for a time, straining our ears as the uncanny rhythm seemed more and more to take on a vital quality. Then without apparent volition we began to move toward the door, whose rattling in the gale held a comforting suggestion of earthly reality. The chanting in the depths - for such the sound now seemed to be - grew in volume and distinctness; and we felt irresistibly urged out into the storm and thence to the gaping blackness of the shaft.

We encountered no living creature, for the men of the night shift had been released from duty, and were doubtless at the Dry Gulch settlement pouring sinister rumors into the ear of some drowsy bartender. From the watchman's cabin, however, gleamed a small square of yellow light like a guardian eye. I dimly wondered how the rhythmic sound had affected the watchman; but Romero was moving more swiftly now, and I followed without pausing.

As we descended the shaft, the sound beneath grew definitely composite. It struck me as horribly like a sort of Oriental ceremony, with beating of drums and chanting of many voices. I have, as you are aware, been much in India. Romero and I moved without material hesitancy through drifts and down ladders; ever toward the thing that allured us, yet ever with a pitifully helpless fear and reluctance. At one time I fancied I had gone mad – this was when, on wondering how our way was lighted in the absence of lamp or candle, I realized that the ancient ring on my finger was glowing with eerie radiance, diffusing a pallid luster through the damp, heavy air around.

It was without warning that Romero, after clambering down one of the many rude ladders, broke into a run and left me alone. Some new and wild note in the drumming and chanting, perceptible but slightly to me, had acted on him in startling fashion; and with a wild outcry he forged ahead unguided in the cavern's gloom. I heard his repeated shrieks before me, as he stumbled awkwardly along the level places and scrambled madly down the rickety ladders. And frightened as I was, I yet retained enough of perception to note that his speech, when articulate, was not of any sort known to me. Harsh but impressive polysyllables had replaced the customary mixture of bad Spanish and worse English, and of these only the oft repeated cry *"Huitzilopotchli"* seemed in the least familiar. Later I definitely placed that word in the works of a great historian – and shuddered when the association came to me.

The climax of that awful night was composite but fairly brief, beginning just as I reached the final cavern of the journey. Out of the darkness immediately ahead burst a final shriek from the Mexican, which was joined by such a chorus of uncouth sound as I could never hear again and survive. In that moment it seemed as if all the hidden terrors and monstrosities of earth had become articulate in an effort to overwhelm the human race. Simultaneously the light from my ring was extinguished, and I saw a new light glimmering from lower space but a few yards ahead of me. I had arrived at the abyss, which was now redly aglow, and which had evidently swallowed up the unfortunate Romero. Advancing, I peered over the edge of that chasm which no line could fathom, and which was now a pandemonium of flickering flame and hideous uproar. At first I beheld nothing but a seething blur of luminosity; but then shapes, all infinitely distant, began to detach themselves from the confusion, and I saw - was it Juan Romero? - *but God! I dare not tell you what I saw!* . . . Some power from heaven, coming to my aid, obliterated both sights and sounds in such a crash as may be heard when two universes collide in space. Chaos supervened, and I knew the peace of oblivion.

I hardly know how to continue, since conditions so singular are involved; but I will do my best, not even trying to differentiate betwixt the real and the apparent. When I awaked, I was safe in my bunk and the red glow of dawn was visible at the window. Some distance away the lifeless body of Juan Romero lay upon a table, surrounded by a group of men, including the camp doctor. The men were discussing the strange death of the Mexican as he lay asleep; a death seemingly connected in some way with the terrible bolt of lightning which had struck and shaken the mountain. No direct cause was evident, and an autopsy failed to shew any reason why Romero should not be living. Snatches of conversation indicated beyond a doubt that neither Romero nor I had left the bunkhouse during the night; that neither had been awake during the frightful storm which had passed over the Cactus range. That storm, said men who had ventured down the mine shaft, had caused extensive caving in, and had completely closed the deep abyss which had created so much apprehension the day before. When I asked the watchman what sounds he had heard prior to the mighty thunderbolt, he mentioned a coyote, a dog, and the snarling mountain wind - nothing more. Nor do I doubt his word.

Upon the resumption of work Superintendent Arthur called on some especially dependable men to make a few investigations around the spot where the gulf had appeared. Though hardly eager, they obeyed; and a deep boring was made. Results were very curious. The roof of the void, as seen whilst it was open, was not by any means thick; yet now the drills of the investigators met what appeared to be a limitless extent of solid rock. Finding nothing else, not even gold, the Superintendent abandoned his attempts; but a perplexed look occasionally steals over his countenance as he sits thinking at his desk.

One other thing is curious. Shortly after waking on that morning after the storm, I noticed the unaccountable absence of my Hindoo ring from my finger. I had prized it greatly, yet nevertheless felt a sensation of relief at its disappearance. If one of my fellow-miners appropriated it, he must have been quite clever in disposing of his booty, for despite advertisements and a police search the ring was never seen again. Somehow I doubt if it was stolen by mortal hands, for many strange things were taught me in India.

My opinion of my whole experience varies from time to time. In broad daylight, and at most seasons I am apt to think the greater part of it a mere dream; but sometimes in the autumn, about two in the morning when winds and animals howl dismally, there comes from inconceivable depths below a damnable suggestion of rhythmical throbbing . . . and I feel that the transition of Juan Romero was a terrible one indeed.

THE TERRIBLE OLD MAN

It was the design of Angelo Ricci and Joe Czanek and Manuel Silva to call on the Terrible Old Man. This old man dwells all alone in a very ancient house on Water Street near the sea, and is reputed to be both exceedingly rich and exceedingly feeble; which forms a situation very attractive to men of the profession of Messrs. Ricci, Czanek, and Silva, for that profession was nothing less dignified than robbery.

The inhabitants of Kingsport say and think many things about the Terrible Old Man which generally keep him safe from the attention of gentlemen like Mr. Ricci and his colleagues, despite the almost certain fact that he hides a fortune of indefinite magnitude somewhere about his musty and venerable abode. He is, in truth, a very strange person, believed to have been a captain of East India clipper ships in his day; so old that no one can remember when he was young, and so taciturn that few know his real name. Among the gnarled trees in the front yard of his aged and neglected place he maintains a strange collection of large stones, oddly grouped and painted so that they resemble the idols in some obscure Eastern temple. This collection frightens away most of the small boys who love to taunt the Terrible Old Man about his long white hair and beard, or to break the small-paned windows of his dwelling with wicked missiles; but there are other things which frighten the older and more curious folk who sometimes steal up to the house to peer in through the dusty panes. These folk say that on a table in a bare room on the ground floor are many peculiar bottles, in each a small piece of lead suspended pendulum-wise from a string. And they say that the Terrible Old Man talks to these bottles, addressing them by such names as Jack, Scar-Face, Long Tom, Spanish Joe, Peters, and Mate Ellis, and that whenever he speaks to a bottle the little lead pendulum within makes certain definite vibrations as if in answer. Those who have watched the tall, lean, Terrible Old Man in these peculiar conversations, do not watch him again. But Angelo Ricci and Joe Czanek and Manuel Silva were not of Kingsport blood; they were of that new and heterogeneous alien stock which lies outside the charmed circle of New England life and traditions, and they saw in the Terrible Old Man merely a tottering, almost helpless gray-beard, who could not walk without the aid of his knotted cane, and whose thin, weak hands shook pitifully. They were really quite sorry in their way for the lonely, unpopular old fellow, whom everybody shunned, and at whom all the dogs barked singularly. But business is business, and to a robber whose soul is in his profession, there is a lure and a challenge about a very old and very feeble man who has no account at the bank, and who pays for his few necessities at the village store with Spanish gold and silver minted two centuries ago.

Messrs. Ricci, Czanek, and Silva selected the night of April 11th for their call. Mr. Ricci and Mr. Silva were to interview the poor old gentleman, whilst Mr. Czanek waited for them and their presumable metallic burden with a covered motor-car in Ship Street, by the gate in the tall rear wall of their host's grounds. Desire to avoid needless explanations in case of unexpected police intrusions prompted these plans for a quiet and unostentatious departure.

As prearranged, the three adventurers started out separately in order to prevent any evil-minded suspicions afterward. Messrs. Ricci and Silva met in Water Street by the old man's front gate, and although they did not like the way the moon shone down upon the painted stones through the budding branches of the gnarled trees, they had more important things to think about than mere idle superstition. They feared it might be unpleasant work making the Terrible Old Man loquacious concerning his hoarded gold and silver, for aged sea-captains are notably stubborn and perverse. Still, he was very old and very feeble, and there were two visitors. Messrs. Ricci and Silva were experienced in the art of making unwilling persons voluble, and the screams of a weak and exceptionally venerable man can be easily muffled. So they moved up to the one lighted window and heard the Terrible Old Man talking childishly to his bottles with pendulums. Then they donned masks and knocked politely at the weather-stained oaken door.

Waiting seemed very long to Mr. Czanek as he fidgeted restlessly in the covered motor-car by the Terrible Old Man's back gate in Ship Street. He was more than ordinarily tender-hearted, and he did not like the hideous screams he had heard in the ancient house just after the hour appointed for the deed. Had he not told his colleagues to be as gentle as possible with the pathetic old sea-captain? Very nervously he watched that narrow oaken gate in the high and ivy-clad stone wall. Frequently he consulted his watch, and wondered at the delay. Had the old man died before revealing where his treasure was hidden, and had a thorough search become necessary? Mr. Czanek did not like to wait so long in the dark in such a place. Then he sensed a soft tread or tapping on the walk inside the gate, heard a gentle fumbling at the rusty latch, and saw the narrow, heavy door swing inward. And in the pallid glow of the single dim street-lamp he strained his eyes to see what his colleagues had brought out of that sinister house which loomed so close behind. But when he looked, he did not see what he had expected; for his colleagues were not there at all, but only the Terrible Old Man leaning quietly on his knotted cane and smiling hideously. Mr. Czanek had never before noticed the color of that man's eyes; now he saw that they were yellow.

Little things make considerable excitement in little towns, which is the reason that Kingsport people talked all that spring and summer about the three unidentifiable bodies, horribly slashed as with many cutlasses, and horribly mangled as by the tread of many cruel boot-heels, which the tide washed in. And some people even spoke of things as trivial as the deserted motor-car found in Ship Street, or certain especially inhuman cries, probably of a stray animal or migratory bird, heard in the night by wakeful citizens. But in this idle village gossip the Terrible Old Man took no interest at all. He was by nature reserved, and when one is aged and feeble one's reserve is doubly strong. Besides, so ancient a sea-captain must have witnessed scores of things much more stirring in the far-off days of his unremembered youth.

THE TEMPLE

(MANUSCRIPT FOUND ON THE COAST OF YUCATAN)

On August 20, 1917, I, Karl Heinrich, Graf von Altberg-Ehrenstein, Lieutenant-Commander in the Imperial German Navy and in charge of the submarine U-29, deposit this bottle and record in the Atlantic Ocean at a point to me unknown but probably about N. Latitude 20°, W. Longitude 35°, where my ship lies disabled on the ocean floor. I do so because of my desire to set certain unusual facts before the public; a thing I shall not in all probability survive to accomplish in person, since the circumstances surrounding me are as menacing as they are extraordinary, and involve not only the hopeless crippling of the U-29, but the impairment of my iron German will in a manner most disastrous.

On the afternoon of June 18, as reported by wireless to the U-61, bound for Kiel, we torpedoed the British freighter *Victory,* New York to Liverpool, in N. Latitude 45° 16', W. Longitude 28° 34'; permitting the crew to leave in boats in order to obtain a good cinema view for the admiralty records. The ship sank quite picturesquely, bow first, the stern rising high out of the water whilst the hull shot down perpendicularly to the bottom of the sea. Our camera missed nothing, and I regret that so fine a reel of film should never reach Berlin. After that we sank the lifeboats with our guns and submerged.

When we rose to the surface about sunset a seaman's body was found on the deck, hands gripping the railing in curious fashion. The poor fellow was young, rather dark, and very handsome; probably an Italian or Greek, and undoubtedly of the *Victory*'s crew. He had evidently sought refuge on the very ship which had been forced to destroy his own – one more victim of the unjust war of aggression which the English pig-dogs are waging upon the Fatherland. Our men searched him for souvenirs, and found in his coat pocket a very odd bit of ivory carved to represent a youth's head crowned with laurel. My fellow-officer, Lieut. Klenze, believed that the thing was of great age and artistic value, so took it from the men for himself. How it had ever come into the possession of a common sailor, neither he nor I could imagine.

As the dead man was thrown overboard there occurred two incidents which created much disturbance amongst the crew. The fellow's eyes had been closed; but in the dragging of his body to the rail they were jarred open, and many seemed to entertain a queer delusion that they gazed steadily and mockingly at Schmidt and Zimmer, who were bent over the corpse. The Boatswain Müller, an elderly man who would have known better had he not been a superstitious Alsatian swine, became so excited by this impression that he watched the body in the water; and swore that after it sank a little it drew its limbs into a swimming position and sped away to the south under the waves. Klenze and I did not like these displays of peasant ignorance, and severely reprimanded the men, particularly Müller.

The next day a very troublesome situation was created by the indisposition of some of the crew. They were evidently suffering from the nervous strain of our long voyage, and had had bad dreams. Several seemed quite dazed and stupid; and after satisfying myself that they were not feigning their weakness, I excused them from their duties. The sea was rather rough, so we descended to a depth where the waves were less troublesome. Here we were comparatively calm, despite a somewhat puzzling southward current which we could not identify from our ocean-ographic charts. The moans of the sick men were decidedly annoying; but since they did not appear to demoralize the rest of the crew, we did not resort to extreme measures. It was our plan to remain where we were and intercept the liner *Dacia,* mentioned in information from agents in New York.

In the early evening we rose to the surface, and found the sea less heavy. The smoke of a battleship was on the northern horizon, but our distance and ability to submerge made us safe. What worried us more was the talk of Boatswain Müller, which grew wilder as night came on. He was in a detestably childish state, and babbled of some illusion of dead bodies drifting past the undersea portholes; bodies which looked at him intensely, and which he recognized in spite of bloating as having seen dying during some of our victorious German exploits. And he said that the young man we had found and tossed overboard was their leader. This was very gruesome and abnormal, so we confined Müller in irons and had him soundly whipped. The men were not pleased at his punishment, but discipline was necessary. We also denied the request of a delegation headed by Seaman Zimmer, that the curious carved ivory head be cast into the sea.

On June 20, Seamen Bohm and Schmidt, who had been ill the day before, became violently insane. I regretted that no physician was included in our complement of officers, since German lives are precious; but the constant ravings of the two concerning a terrible curse were most subversive of discipline, so drastic steps were taken. The crew accepted the event in a sullen fashion, but it seemed to quiet Müller; who thereafter gave us no trouble. In the evening we released him, and he went about his duties silently.

In the week that followed we were all very nervous, watching for the *Dacia*. The tension was aggravated by the disappearance of Müller and Zimmer, who undoubtedly committed suicide as a result of the fears which had seemed to harass them, though they were not observed in the act of jumping overboard. I was rather glad to be rid of Müller, for even his silence had unfavorably affected the crew. Everyone seemed inclined to be silent now, as though holding a secret fear. Many were ill, but none made a disturbance. Lieut. Klenze chafed under the strain, and was annoyed by the merest trifles – such as the school of dolphins which gathered about the U-29 in increasing numbers, and the growing intensity of that southward current which was not on our chart.

It at length became apparent that we had missed the *Dacia* altogether. Such failures are not uncommon, and we were more pleased than disappointed; since our return to Wilhelmshaven was now in order. At noon June 28 we turned northeastward, and despite some rather comical entanglements with the unusual masses of dolphins were soon under way.

The explosion in the engine room at 2 p.m. was wholly a surprise. No defect in the machinery or carelessness in the men had been noticed, yet without warning the ship was racked from end to end with a colossal shock. Lieut. Klenze hurried to the engine room, finding the fuel-tank and most of the mechanism shattered, and Engineers Raabe and Schneider instantly killed. Our situation had suddenly become grave indeed; for though the chemical air regenerators were intact, and though we could use the devices for raising and submerging the ship and opening the hatches as long as compressed air and storage batteries might hold out, we were powerless to propel or guide the submarine. To seek rescue in the lifeboats would be to deliver ourselves into the hands of enemies unreasonably embittered against our great German nation, and our wireless had failed ever since the *Victory* affair to put us in touch with a fellow U-boat of the Imperial Navy.

From the hour of the accident till July 2 we drifted constantly to the south, almost without plans and encountering no vessel. Dolphins still encircled the U-29, a somewhat remarkable circumstance considering the distance we had covered. On the morning of July 2 we sighted a warship flying American colors, and the men became very restless in their desire to surrender. Finally Lieut. Klenze had to shoot a seaman named Traube, who urged this un-German act with especial violence. This quieted the crew for the time, and we submerged unseen.

The next afternoon a dense flock of sea-birds appeared from the south, and the ocean began to heave ominously. Closing our hatches, we awaited developments until we realized that we must either submerge or be swamped in the mounting waves.

Our air pressure and electricity were diminishing, and we wished to avoid all unnecessary use of our slender mechanical resources; but in this case there was no choice. We did not descend far, and when after several hours the sea was calmer, we decided to return to the surface. Here, however, a new trouble developed; for the ship failed to respond to our direction in spite of all that the mechanics could do. As the men grew more frightened at this undersea imprisonment, some of them began to mutter again about Lieut. Klenze's ivory image, but the sight of an automatic pistol calmed them. We kept the poor devils as busy as we could, tinkering at the machinery even when we knew it was useless.

Klenze and I usually slept at different times; and it was during my sleep, about 5 a.m., July 4, that the general mutiny broke loose. The six remaining pigs of seamen, suspecting that we were lost, had suddenly burst into a mad fury at our refusal to surrender to the Yankee battleship two days before; and were in a delirium of cursing and destruction. They roared like the animals they were, and broke instruments and furniture indiscriminately; screaming about such nonsense as the curse of the ivory image and the dark dead youth who looked at them and swam away. Lieut. Klenze seemed paralyzed and inefficient, as one might expect of a soft, womanish Rhinelander. I shot all six men, for it was necessary, and made sure that none remained alive.

We expelled the bodies through the double hatches and were alone in the U-29. Klenze seemed very nervous, and drank heavily. It was decided that we remain alive as long as possible, using the large stock of provisions and chemical supply of oxygen, none of which had suffered from the crazy antics of those swine-hound seamen. Our compasses, depth gauges, and other delicate instruments were ruined; so that henceforth our only reckoning would be guesswork, based on our watches, the calendar, and our apparent drift as judged by any objects we might spy through the portholes or from the conning tower. Fortunately we had storage batteries still capable of long use, both for interior lighting and for the searchlight. We often cast a beam around the ship, but saw only dolphins, swimming parallel to our own drifting course. I was scientifically interested in those dolphins; for though the ordinary *Delphinus delphis* is a cetacean mammal, unable to subsist without air, I watched one of the swimmers closely for two hours, and did not see him alter his submerged condition.

With the passage of time Klenze and I decided that we were still drifting south, meanwhile sinking deeper and deeper. We noted the marine fauna and flora, and read much on the subject in the books I had carried with me for spare moments. I could not help observing, however, the inferior scientific knowledge of my companion. His mind was not Prussian, but given to imaginings and speculations which have no value. The fact of our coming death affected him curiously, and he would frequently pray in remorse over the men, women, and children we had sent to the bottom; forgetting that all things are noble which serve the German state. After a time he became noticeably unbalanced, gazing for hours at his ivory image and weaving fanciful stories of the lost and forgotten things under the sea. Sometimes, as a psychological experiment, I would lead him on in these wanderings, and listen to his endless poetical quotations and tales of sunken ships. I was very sorry for him, for I dislike to see a German suffer; but he was not a good man to die with. For myself I was proud, knowing how the Fatherland would revere my memory and how my sons would be taught to be men like me.

On August 9, we espied the ocean floor, and sent a powerful beam from the searchlight over it. It was a vast undulating plain, mostly covered with seaweed, and strown with the shells of small mollusks. Here and there were slimy objects of puzzling contour, draped with weeds and encrusted with barnacles, which Klenze declared must be ancient ships lying in their graves. He was puzzled by one thing, a peak of solid matter, protruding above the ocean bed nearly four feet at its apex; about two feet thick, with flat sides and smooth upper surfaces which met at a very obtuse angle. I called the peak a bit of outcropping rock, but Klenze thought he saw carvings on it. After a while he began to shudder, and turned away from the scene as if frightened; yet could give no explanation save that he was overcome with the vastness, darkness, remoteness, antiquity, and mystery of the oceanic abysses. His mind was tired, but I am always a German, and was quick to notice two things; that the U-29 was standing the deep-sea pressure splendidly, and that the peculiar dolphins were still about us, even at a depth where the existence of high organisms is considered impossible by most naturalists. That I had previously overestimated our depth, I was sure; but none the less we must still be deep enough to make these phenomena remarkable. Our southward speed, as gauged by the ocean floor, was about as I had estimated from the organisms passed at higher levels.

It was at 3:15 p.m., August 12, that poor Klenze went wholly mad. He had been in the conning tower using the searchlight when I saw him bound into the library compartment where I sat reading, and his face at once betrayed him. I will repeat here what he said, underlining the words he emphasized: "*He* is calling! *He* is calling! I hear him! We must go!" As he spoke he took his ivory image from the table, pocketed it, and seized my arm in an effort to drag me up the companionway to the deck. In a moment I understood that he meant to open the hatch and plunge with me into the water outside, a vagary of suicidal and homicidal mania for which I was scarcely prepared. As I hung back and attempted to soothe him he grew more violent, saying: "Come now – do not wait until later; it is better to repent and be forgiven than to defy and be condemned." Then I tried the opposite of the soothing plan, and told him he was mad – pitifully demented. But he was unmoved, and cried: "If I am mad, it is mercy! May the gods pity the man who in his callousness can remain sane to the hideous end! Come and be mad whilst *he* still calls with mercy!"

This outburst seemed to relieve a pressure in his brain; for as he finished he grew much milder, asking me to let him depart alone if I would not accompany him. My course at once became clear. He was a German, but only a Rhinelander and a commoner; and he was now a potentially dangerous madman. By complying with his suicidal request I could immediately free myself from one who was no longer a companion but a menace. I asked him to give me the ivory image before he went, but this request brought from him such uncanny laughter that I did not repeat it. Then I asked him if he wished to leave any keepsake or lock of hair for his family in Germany in case I should be rescued, but again he gave me that strange laugh. So as he climbed the ladder I went to the levers, and allowing proper time-intervals operated the machinery which sent him to his death. After I saw that he was no longer in the boat I threw the searchlight around the water in an effort to obtain a last glimpse of him; since I wished to ascertain whether the water-pressure would flatten him as it theoretically should, or whether the body would be unaffected, like those extraordinary dolphins. I did not, however, succeed in finding my late companion, for the dolphins were massed thickly and obscuringly about the conning tower.

That evening I regretted that I had not taken the ivory image surreptitiously from poor Klenze's pocket as he left, for the memory of it fascinated me. I could not forget the youthful, beautiful head with its leafy crown, though I am not by nature an artist. I was also sorry that I had no one with whom to converse. Klenze, though not my mental equal, was much better than no one. I did not sleep well that night, and wondered exactly when the end would come. Surely, I had little enough chance of rescue.

The next day I ascended to the conning tower and commenced the customary searchlight explorations. Northward the view was much the same as it had been all the four days since we had sighted the bottom, but I perceived that the drifting of the U-29 was less rapid. As I swung the beam around to the south, I noticed that the ocean floor ahead fell away in a marked declivity, and bore curiously regular blocks of stone in certain places, disposed as if in accordance with definite patterns. The boat did not at once descend to match the greater ocean depth, so I was soon forced to adjust the searchlight to cast a sharply downward beam. Owing to the abruptness of the change a wire was disconnected, which necessitated a delay of many minutes for repairs; but at length the light streamed on again, flooding the marine valley below me.

I am not given to emotion of any kind, but my amazement was very great when I saw what lay revealed in that electrical glow. And yet as one reared in the best *Kultur* of Prussia I should not have been amazed, for geology and tradition alike tell us of great transpositions in oceanic and continental areas. What I saw was an extended and elaborate array of ruined edifices; all of magnificent though unclassified architecture, and in various stages of preservation. Most appeared to be of marble, gleaming whitely in the rays of the searchlight, and the general plan was of a large city at the bottom of a narrow valley, with numerous isolated temples and villas on the steep slopes above. Roofs were fallen and columns were broken, but there still remained an air of immemorially ancient splendor which nothing could efface.

Confronted at last with the Atlantis I had formerly deemed largely a myth, I was the most eager of explorers. At the bottom of that valley a river once had flowed; for as I examined the scene more closely I beheld the remains of stone and marble bridges and sea-walls, and terraces and embankments once verdant and beautiful. In my enthusiasm I became nearly as idiotic and sentimental as poor Klenze, and was very tardy in noticing that the southward current had ceased at last, allowing the U-29 to settle slowly down upon the sunken city as an aëroplane settles upon a town of the upper earth. I was slow, too, in realizing that the school of unusual dolphins had vanished.

In about two hours the boat rested in a paved plaza close to the rocky wall of the valley. On one side I could view the entire city as it sloped from the plaza down to the old river-bank; on the other side, in startling proximity, I was confronted by the richly ornate and perfectly preserved facade of a great building, evidently a temple, hollowed from the solid rock. Of the original workmanship of this titanic thing I can only make conjectures. The facade, of immense magnitude, apparently covers a continuous hollow recess; for its windows are many and widely distributed. In the center yawns a great open door, reached by an impressive flight of steps, and surrounded by exquisite carvings like the figures of Bacchanals in relief. Foremost of all are the great columns and frieze, both decorated with sculptures of inexpressible beauty; obviously portraying idealized pastoral scenes and processions of priests and priestesses bearing strange ceremonial devices in adoration of a radiant god. The art is of the most phenomenal perfection, largely Hellenic in idea, yet strangely individual. It imparts an impression of terrible antiquity, as though it were the remotest rather than the immediate ancestor of Greek art. Nor can I doubt that every detail of this massive product was fashioned from the virgin hillside rock of our planet. It is palpably a part of the valley wall, though how the vast interior was ever excavated I cannot imagine. Perhaps a cavern or series of caverns furnished the nucleus. Neither age nor submersion has corroded the pristine grandeur of this awful fane – for fane indeed it must be – and today after thousands of years it rests untarnished and inviolate in the endless night and silence of an ocean chasm.

I cannot reckon the number of hours I spent in gazing at the sunken city with its buildings, arches, statues, and bridges, and the colossal temple with its beauty and mystery. Though I knew that death was near, my curiosity was consuming; and I threw the searchlight's beam about in eager quest. The shaft of light permitted me to learn many details, but refused to shew anything within the gaping door of the rock-hewn temple; and after a time I turned off the current, conscious of the need of conserving power. The rays were now perceptibly dimmer than they had been during the weeks of drifting. And as if sharpened by the coming deprivation of light, my desire to explore the watery

secrets grew. I, a German, should be the first to tread those
eon-forgotten ways!

I produced and examined a deep-sea diving suit of joined
metal, and experimented with the portable light and air regenerator. Though I should have trouble in managing the double
hatches alone, I believed I could overcome all obstacles with my
scientific skill and actually walk about the dead city in person.

On August 16 I effected an exit from the U-29, and laboriously
made my way through the ruined and mud-choked streets to the
ancient river. I found no skeletons or other human remains, but
gleaned a wealth of archeological lore from sculptures and coins.
Of this I cannot now speak save to utter my awe at a culture in
the full noon of glory when cave-dwellers roamed Europe and
the Nile flowed unwatched to the sea. Others, guided by this
manuscript if it shall ever be found, must unfold the mysteries
at which I can only hint. I returned to the boat as my electric
batteries grew feeble, resolved to explore the rock temple on
the following day.

On the 17th, as my impulse to search out the mystery of the
temple waxed still more insistent, a great disappointment befell
me; for I found that the materials needed to replenish the portable light had perished in the mutiny of those pigs in July. My
rage was unbounded, yet my German sense forbade me to venture
unprepared into an utterly black interior which might prove the
lair of some indescribable marine monster or a labyrinth of
passages from whose windings I could never extricate myself.
All I could do was to turn on the waning searchlight of the U-29,
and with its aid walk up the temple steps and study the exterior
carvings. The shaft of light entered the door at an upward angle,
and I peered in to see if I could glimpse anything, but all in vain.
Not even the roof was visible; and though I took a step or two
inside after testing the floor with a staff, I dared not go farther.
Moreover, for the first time in my life I experienced the emotion
of dread. I began to realize how some of poor Klenze's moods
had arisen, for as the temple drew me more and more, I feared

its aqueous abysses with a blind and mounting terror. Returning to the submarine, I turned off the lights and sat thinking in the dark. Electricity must now be saved for emergencies.

Saturday the 18th I spent in total darkness, tormented by thoughts and memories that threatened to overcome my German will. Klenze had gone mad and perished before reaching this sinister remnant of a past unwholesomely remote, and had advised me to go with him. Was, indeed, Fate preserving my reason only to draw me irresistibly to an end more horrible and unthinkable than any man has dreamed of? Clearly, my nerves were sorely taxed, and I must cast off these impressions of weaker men.

I could not sleep Saturday night, and turned on the lights regardless of the future. It was annoying that the electricity should not last out the air and provisions. I revived my thoughts of euthanasia, and examined my automatic pistol. Toward morning I must have dropped asleep with the lights on, for I awoke in darkness yesterday afternoon to find the batteries dead. I struck several matches in succession, and desperately regretted the improvidence which had caused us long ago to use up the few candles we carried.

After the fading of the last match I dared to waste, I sat very quietly without a light. As I considered the inevitable end my mind ran over preceding events, and developed a hitherto dormant impression which would have caused a weaker and more superstitious man to shudder. *The head of the radiant god in the sculptures on the rock temple is the same as that carven bit of ivory which the dead sailor brought from the sea and which poor Klenze carried back into the sea.*

I was a little dazed by this coincidence, but did not become terrified. It is only the inferior thinker who hastens to explain the singular and the complex by the primitive short cut of supernaturalism. The coincidence was strange, but I was too sound a reasoner to connect circumstances which admit of no logical connexion, or to associate in any uncanny fashion the disastrous events which had led from the *Victory* affair to my present plight. Feeling the need of more rest, I took a sedative and secured some more sleep. My nervous condition was reflected in my dreams, for I seemed to hear the cries of drowning persons, and to see dead faces pressing against the portholes of the boat. And among the dead faces was the living, mocking face of the youth with the ivory image.

I must be careful how I record my awaking today, for I am unstrung, and much hallucination is necessarily mixed with fact. Psychologically my case is most interesting, and I regret that it cannot be observed scientifically by a competent German authority. Upon opening my eyes my first sensation was an over-mastering desire to visit the rock temple; a desire which grew every instant, yet which I automatically sought to resist through some emotion of fear which operated in the reverse direction. Next there came to me the impression of *light* amidst the dark-ness of dead batteries, and I seemed to see a sort of phosphorescent glow in the water through the porthole which opened toward the temple. This aroused my curiosity, for I knew of no deep-sea organism capable of emitting such luminosity. But before I could investigate there came a third impression which because of its irrationality caused me to doubt the objec-tivity of anything my senses might record. It was an aural delusion; a sensation of rhythmic, melodic sound as of some wild yet beautiful chant or choral hymn, coming from the outside through the absolutely sound-proof hull of the U-29. Convinced of my psychological and nervous abnormality, I lighted some matches and poured a stiff dose of sodium bromide solution, which seemed to calm me to the extent of dispelling the illusion of sound. But the phosphorescence remained, and I had difficulty in repressing a childish impulse to go to the porthole and seek its source. It was horribly realistic, and I could soon distinguish by its aid the familiar objects around me, as well as the empty sodium bromide glass of which I had had no former visual impression in its present location. The last circumstance made me ponder, and I crossed the room and touched the glass. It was indeed in the place where I had seemed to see it. Now I knew that the light was either real or part of an hallucination so fixed and consistent that I could not hope to dispel it, so abandoning all resistance I ascended to the conning tower to look for the luminous agency. Might it not actually be another U-boat, offering possibilities of rescue?

It is well that the reader accept nothing which follows as objective truth, for since the events transcend natural law, they are necessarily the subjective and unreal creations of my over-taxed mind. When I attained the conning tower I found the sea in general far less luminous than I had expected. There was no animal or vegetable phosphorescence about, and the city that sloped down to the river was invisible in blackness. What I did see was not spectacular, not grotesque or terrifying, yet it removed my last vestige of trust in my consciousness. *For the door and windows of the undersea temple hewn from the rocky hill were vividly aglow with a flickering radiance, as from a mighty altar-flame far within.*

Later incidents are chaotic. As I stared at the uncannily lighted door and windows, I became subject to the most extravagant visions – visions so extravagant that I cannot even relate them. I fancied that I discerned objects in the temple – objects both stationary and moving – and seemed to hear again the unreal chant that had floated to me when first I awaked. And over all rose thoughts and fears which centered in the youth from the sea and the ivory image whose carving was duplicated on the frieze and columns of the temple before me. I thought of poor Klenze, and wondered where his body rested with the image he had carried back into the sea. He had warned me of something, and I had not heeded – but he was a soft-headed Rhinelander who went mad at troubles a Prussian could bear with ease.

The rest is very simple. My impulse to visit and enter the temple has now become an inexplicable and imperious command which ultimately cannot be denied. My own German will no longer controls my acts, and volition is henceforward possible

only in minor matters. Such madness it was which drove Klenze
to his death, bareheaded and unprotected in the ocean; but I am
a Prussian and a man of sense, and will use to the last what little
will I have. When first I saw that I must go, I prepared my diving
suit, helmet, and air regenerator for instant donning; and immediately commenced to write this hurried chronicle in the hope
that it may some day reach the world. I shall seal the manuscript
in a bottle and entrust it to the sea as I leave the U-29 forever.

I have no fear, not even from the prophecies of the madman
Klenze. What I have seen cannot be true, and I know that this
madness of my own will at most lead only to suffocation when
my air is gone. The light in the temple is a sheer delusion, and
I shall die calmly, like a German, in the black and forgotten
depths. This daemoniac laughter which I hear as I write comes
only from my own weakening brain. So I will carefully don my
diving suit and walk boldly up the steps into that primal shrine;
that silent secret of unfathomed waters and uncounted years.

FACTS CONCERNING THE
LATE ARTHUR JERMYN
AND HIS FAMILY

I

Life is a hideous thing, and from the background behind what we know of it peer daemoniacal hints of truth which make it sometimes a thousandfold more hideous. Science, already oppressive with its shocking revelations, will perhaps be the ultimate exterminator of our human species – if separate species we be – for its reserve of unguessed horrors could never be borne by mortal brains if loosed upon the world. If we knew what we are, we should do as Sir Arthur Jermyn did; and Arthur Jermyn soaked himself in oil and set fire to his clothing one night. No one placed the charred fragments in an urn or set a memorial to him who had been; for certain papers and a certain boxed *object* were found, which made men wish to forget. Some who knew him do not admit that he ever existed.

Arthur Jermyn went out on the moor and burned himself after seeing the boxed *object* which had come from Africa. It was this *object,* and not his peculiar personal appearance, which made him end his life. Many would have disliked to live if possessed of the peculiar features of Arthur Jermyn, but he had been a poet and scholar and had not minded. Learning was in his blood, for his great-grandfather, Sir Robert Jermyn, Bt., had been an anthropologist of note, whilst his great-great-great-grandfather, Sir Wade Jermyn, was one of the earliest explorers of the Congo region, and had written eruditely of its tribes, animals, and supposed antiquities. Indeed, old Sir Wade had possessed an intellectual zeal amounting almost to a mania; his bizarre conjectures on a prehistoric white Congolese civilization earning him much ridicule when his book, *Observations on the Several Parts of Africa,* was published. In 1765 this fearless explorer had been placed in a madhouse at Huntingdon.

Madness was in all the Jermyns, and people were glad there were not many of them. The line put forth no branches, and Arthur was the last of it. If he had not been, one cannot say what he would have done when the *object* came. The Jermyns never seemed to look quite right – something was amiss, though Arthur was the worst, and the old family portraits in Jermyn House shewed fine faces enough before Sir Wade's time. Certainly, the madness began with Sir Wade, whose wild stories of Africa were at once the delight and terror of his few friends. It shewed in his collection of trophies and specimens, which were not such as a normal man would accumulate and preserve, and appeared strikingly in the Oriental seclusion in which he kept his wife. The latter, he had said, was the daughter of a Portuguese trader whom he had met in Africa; and did not like English ways. She, with an infant son born in Africa, had accompanied him back from the second and longest of his trips, and had gone with him on the third and last, never returning. No one had ever seen her closely, not even the servants; for her disposition had been violent and singular. During her brief stay at Jermyn House she occupied a remote wing, and was waited on by her husband alone. Sir Wade was, indeed, most peculiar in his solicitude for his family; for when he returned to Africa he would permit no one to care for his young son save a loathsome black woman from Guinea. Upon coming back, after the death of Lady Jermyn, he himself assumed complete care of the boy.

But it was the talk of Sir Wade, especially when in his cups, which chiefly led his friends to deem him mad. In a rational age like the eighteenth century it was unwise for a man of learning to talk about wild sights and strange scenes under a Congo moon;

of the gigantic walls and pillars of a forgotten city, crumbling and vine-grown, and of damp, silent, stone steps leading interminably down into the darkness of abysmal treasure-vaults and inconceivable catacombs. Especially was it unwise to rave of the living things that might haunt such a place; of creatures half of the jungle and half of the impiously aged city – fabulous creatures which even a Pliny might describe with skepticism; things that might have sprung up after the great apes had overrun the dying city with the walls and the pillars, the vaults and the weird carvings. Yet after he came home for the last time Sir Wade would speak of such matters with a shudderingly uncanny zest, mostly after his third glass at the Knight's Head; boasting of what he had found in the jungle and of how he had dwelt among terrible ruins known only to him. And finally he had spoken of the living things in such a manner that he was taken to the madhouse. He had shewn little regret when shut into the barred room at Huntingdon, for his mind moved curiously. Ever since his son had commenced to grow out of infancy he had liked his home less and less, till at last he had seemed to dread it. The Knight's Head had been his headquarters, and when he was confined he expressed some vague gratitude as if for protection. Three years later he died.

Wade Jermyn's son Philip was a highly peculiar person. Despite a strong physical resemblance to his father, his appearance and conduct were in many particulars so coarse that he was universally shunned. Though he did not inherit the madness which was feared by some, he was densely stupid and given to brief periods of uncontrollable violence. In frame he was small, but intensely powerful, and was of incredible agility. Twelve years after succeeding to his title he married the daughter of his gamekeeper, a person said to be of gypsy extraction, but before his son was born joined the navy as a common sailor, completing the general disgust which his habits and mesalliance had begun. After the close of the American war he was heard of as a sailor on a merchantman in the African trade, having a kind of reputation for feats of strength and climbing, but finally disappearing one night as his ship lay off the Congo coast.

In the son of Sir Philip Jermyn the now accepted family peculiarity took a strange and fatal turn. Tall and fairly handsome, with a sort of weird Eastern grace despite certain slight oddities of proportion, Robert Jermyn began life as a scholar and investigator. It was he who first studied scientifically the vast collection of relics which his mad grandfather had brought from Africa, and who made the family name as celebrated in ethnology as in exploration. In 1815 Sir Robert married a daughter of the seventh Viscount Brightholme and was subsequently blessed with three children, the eldest and youngest of whom were never publicly seen on account of deformities in mind and body. Saddened by these family misfortunes, the scientist sought relief in work, and made two long expeditions in the interior of Africa. In 1849 his second son, Nevil, a singularly repellent person who seemed to combine the surliness of Philip Jermyn with the hauteur of the Brightholmes, ran away with a vulgar dancer, but was pardoned upon his return in the following year. He came back to Jermyn House a widower with an infant son, Alfred, who was one day to be the father of Arthur Jermyn.

Friends said that it was this series of griefs which unhinged the mind of Sir Robert Jermyn, yet it was probably merely a bit of African folklore which caused the disaster. The elderly scholar had been collecting legends of the Onga tribes near the field of his grandfather's and his own explorations, hoping in some way to account for Sir Wade's wild tales of a lost city peopled by strange hybrid creatures. A certain consistency in the strange papers of his ancestor suggested that the madman's imagination might have been stimulated by native myths. On October 19, 1852, the explorer Samuel Seaton called at Jermyn House with a manuscript of notes collected among the Ongas, believing that certain legends of a gray city of white apes ruled by a white god might prove valuable to the ethnologist. In his conversation he probably supplied many additional details; the nature of which will never be known, since a hideous series of tragedies suddenly burst into being. When Sir Robert Jermyn emerged from his library he left behind the strangled corpse of the explorer, and before he could be restrained, had put an end to all three of his children; the two who were never seen, and the son who had run away. Nevil Jermyn died in the successful defense of his own two-year-old son, who had apparently been included in the old man's madly murderous scheme. Sir Robert himself, after repeated attempts at suicide and a stubborn refusal to utter any articulate sound, died of apoplexy in the second year of his confinement.

Sir Alfred Jermyn was a baronet before his fourth birthday, but his tastes never matched his title. At twenty he had joined a band of music-hall performers, and at thirty-six had deserted his wife and child to travel with an itinerant American circus. His end was very revolting. Among the animals in the exhibition with which he traveled was a huge bull gorilla of lighter color than the average; a surprisingly tractable beast of much popularity with the performers. With this gorilla Alfred Jermyn was singularly fascinated, and on many occasions the two would eye each other for long periods through the intervening bars. Eventually Jermyn asked and obtained permission to train the animal, astonishing audiences and fellow-performers alike with his success. One morning in Chicago, as the gorilla and Alfred Jermyn were rehearsing an exceedingly clever boxing match, the former delivered a blow of more than usual force, hurting both the body and dignity of the amateur trainer. Of what followed, members of "The Greatest Show on Earth" do not like to speak. They did not expect to hear Sir Alfred Jermyn emit a shrill, inhuman scream, or to see him seize his clumsy antagonist with both hands, dash it to the floor of the cage, and bite fiendishly at its hairy throat. The gorilla was off its guard, but not for long, and before anything could be done by the regular trainer the body which had belonged to a baronet was past recognition.

II

Arthur Jermyn was the son of Sir Alfred Jermyn and a music-hall singer of unknown origin. When the husband and father deserted his family, the mother took the child to Jermyn House; where there was none left to object to her presence. She was not without notions of what a nobleman's dignity should be, and saw to it that her son received the best education which limited money could provide. The family resources were now sadly slender, and Jermyn House had fallen into woeful disrepair, but young Arthur loved the old edifice and all its contents. He was not like any other Jermyn who had ever lived, for he was a poet and a dreamer. Some of the neighboring families who had heard tales of old Sir Wade Jermyn's unseen Portuguese wife declared that her Latin blood must be shewing itself; but most persons merely sneered at his sensitiveness to beauty, attributing it to his music-hall mother, who was socially unrecognized. The poetic delicacy of Arthur Jermyn was the more remarkable because of his uncouth personal appearance. Most of the Jermyns had possessed a subtly odd and repellent cast, but Arthur's case was very striking. It is hard to say just what he resembled, but his expression, his facial angle, and the length of his arms gave a thrill of repulsion to those who met him for the first time.

It was the mind and character of Arthur Jermyn which atoned for his aspect. Gifted and learned, he took highest honors at Oxford and seemed likely to redeem the intellectual fame of his family. Though of poetic rather than scientific temperament, he planned to continue the work of his forefathers in African ethnology and antiquities, utilizing the truly wonderful though strange collection of Sir Wade. With his fanciful mind he thought often of the prehistoric civilization in which the mad explorer had so implicitly believed, and would weave tale after tale about the silent jungle city mentioned in the latter's wilder notes and paragraphs. For the nebulous utterances concerning a nameless, unsuspected race of jungle hybrids he had a peculiar feeling of mingled terror and attraction; speculating on the possible basis of such a fancy, and seeking to obtain light among the more recent data gleaned by his great-grandfather and Samuel Seaton amongst the Ongas.

In 1911, after the death of his mother, Sir Arthur Jermyn determined to pursue his investigations to the utmost extent. Selling a portion of his estate to obtain the requisite money, he outfitted an expedition and sailed for the Congo. Arranging with the Belgian authorities for a party of guides, he spent a year in the Onga and Kaliri country, finding data beyond the highest of his expectations. Among the Kaliris was an aged chief called Mwanu, who possessed not only a highly retentive memory, but a singular degree of intelligence and interest in old legends. This ancient confirmed every tale which Jermyn had heard, adding his own account of the stone city and the white apes as it had been told to him.

According to Mwanu, the gray city and the hybrid creatures were no more, having been annihilated by the warlike N'bangus many years ago. This tribe, after destroying most of the edifices and killing the live beings, had carried off the stuffed goddess which had been the object of their quest; the white ape-goddess which the strange beings worshiped, and which was held by Congo tradition to be the form of one who had reigned as a princess among those beings. Just what the white ape-like creatures could have been, Mwanu had no idea, but he thought they were the builders of the ruined city. Jermyn could form no conjecture, but by close questioning obtained a very picturesque legend of the stuffed goddess.

The ape-princess, it was said, became the consort of a great white god who had come out of the West. For a long time they had reigned over the city together, but when they had a son all three went away. Later the god and the princess had returned, and upon the death of the princess her divine husband had mummified the body and enshrined it in a vast house of stone, where it was worshiped. Then he had departed alone. The legend here seemed to present three variants. According to one story nothing further happened save that the stuffed goddess became a symbol of supremacy for whatever tribe might possess it. It was for this reason that the N'bangus carried it off. A second story told of the god's return and death at the feet of his enshrined wife. A third told of the return of the son, grown to manhood – or apehood or godhood, as the case might be – yet unconscious of his identity. Surely the imaginative blacks had made the most of whatever events might lie behind the extravagant legendry.

Of the reality of the jungle city described by old Sir Wade, Arthur Jermyn had no further doubt; and was hardly astonished when early in 1912 he came upon what was left of it. Its size must have been exaggerated, yet the stones lying about proved that it was no mere negro village. Unfortunately no carvings could be found, and the small size of the expedition prevented operations toward clearing the one visible passageway that seemed to lead down into the system of vaults which Sir Wade had mentioned. The white apes and the stuffed goddess were discussed with all the native chiefs of the region, but it remained for a European to improve on the data offered by old Mwanu. M. Verhaeren, Belgian agent at a trading-post on the Congo, believed that he could not only locate but obtain the stuffed goddess, of which he had vaguely heard; since the once mighty N'bangus were now the submissive servants of King Albert's government, and with but little persuasion could be induced to part with the gruesome deity they had carried off. When Jermyn sailed for England, therefore, it was with the exultant probability that he would within a few months receive a priceless ethnological relic confirming the wildest of his great-great-great-grandfather's narratives – that is, the wildest which he had ever heard. Countrymen near Jermyn House had perhaps heard wilder tales handed down from ancestors who had listened to Sir Wade around the tables of the Knight's Head.

Arthur Jermyn waited very patiently for the expected box from M. Verhaeren, meanwhile studying with increased diligence

the manuscripts left by his mad ancestor. He began to feel closely
akin to Sir Wade, and to seek relics of the latter's personal life in
England as well as of his African exploits. Oral accounts of the
mysterious and secluded wife had been numerous, but no tangible
relic of her stay at Jermyn House remained. Jermyn wondered
what circumstance had prompted or permitted such an efface-
ment, and decided that the husband's insanity was the prime
cause. His great-great-great-grandmother, he recalled, was said to
have been the daughter of a Portuguese trader in Africa. No doubt
her practical heritage and superficial knowledge of the Dark
Continent had caused her to flout Sir Wade's talk of the interior,
a thing which such a man would not be likely to forgive. She had
died in Africa, perhaps dragged thither by a husband determined
to prove what he had told. But as Jermyn indulged in these
reflections he could not but smile at their futility, a century and
a half after the death of both of his strange progenitors.

In June, 1913, a letter arrived from M. Verhaeren, telling of
the finding of the stuffed goddess. It was, the Belgian averred,
a most extraordinary object; an object quite beyond the power
of a layman to classify. Whether it was human or simian only a
scientist could determine, and the process of determination
would be greatly hampered by its imperfect condition. Time and
the Congo climate are not kind to mummies; especially when
their preparation is as amateurish as seemed to be the case here.
Around the creature's neck had been found a golden chain
bearing an empty locket on which were armorial designs; no
doubt some hapless traveler's keepsake, taken by the N'bangus
and hung upon the goddess as a charm. In commenting on the
contour of the mummy's face, M. Verhaeren suggested a whim-
sical comparison; or rather, expressed a humorous wonder just
how it would strike his correspondent, but was too much interested scientifically to waste many words in levity. The stuffed
goddess, he wrote, would arrive duly packed about a month
after receipt of the letter.

The boxed object was delivered at Jermyn House on the

afternoon of August 3, 1913, being conveyed immediately to the large chamber which housed the collection of African specimens as arranged by Sir Robert and Arthur. What ensued can best be gathered from the tales of servants and from things and papers later examined. Of the various tales that of aged Soames, the family butler, is most ample and coherent. According to this trustworthy man, Sir Arthur Jermyn dismissed everyone from the room before opening the box, though the instant sound of hammer and chisel shewed that he did not delay the operation. Nothing was heard for some time; just how long Soames cannot exactly estimate; but it was certainly less than a quarter of an hour later that the horrible scream, undoubtedly in Jermyn's voice, was heard. Immediately afterward Jermyn emerged from the room, rushing frantically toward the front of the house as if pursued by some hideous enemy. The expression on his face, a face ghastly enough in repose, was beyond description. When near the front door he seemed to think of something, and turned back in his flight, finally disappearing down the stairs to the cellar. The servants were utterly dumbfounded, and watched at the head of the stairs, but their master did not return. A smell of oil was all that came up from the regions below. After dark a rattling was heard at the door leading from the cellar into the courtyard; and a stable-boy saw Arthur Jermyn, glistening from head to foot with oil and redolent of that fluid, steal furtively out and vanish on the black moor surrounding the house. Then, in an exaltation of supreme horror, everyone saw the end. A spark appeared on the moor, a flame arose, and a pillar of human fire reached to the heavens. The house of Jermyn no longer existed.

The reason why Arthur Jermyn's charred fragments were not collected and buried lies in what was found afterward, principally the thing in the box. The stuffed goddess was a nauseous sight, withered and eaten away, but it was clearly a mummified white ape of some unknown species, less hairy than any recorded variety, and infinitely nearer mankind – quite shockingly so. Detailed description would be rather unpleasant, but two salient particulars must be told, for they fit in revoltingly with certain notes of Sir Wade Jermyn's African expeditions and with the Congolese legends of the white god and the ape-princess. The two particulars in question are these: the arms on the golden locket about the creature's neck were the Jermyn arms, and the jocose suggestion of M. Verhaeren about a certain resemblance as connected with the shriveled face applied with vivid, ghastly, and unnatural horror to none other than the sensitive Arthur Jermyn, great-great-great-grandson of Sir Wade Jermyn and an unknown wife. Members of the Royal Anthropological Institute burned the thing and threw the locket into a well, and some of them do not admit that Arthur Jermyn ever existed.

THE STREET

There be those who say that things and places have souls, and there be those who say they have not; I dare not say, myself, but I will tell of The Street.

Men of strength and honor fashioned that Street; good, valiant men of our blood who had come from the Blessed Isles across the sea. At first it was but a path trodden by bearers of water from the woodland spring to the cluster of houses by the beach. Then, as more men came to the growing cluster of houses and looked about for places to dwell, they built cabins along the north side; cabins of stout oaken logs with masonry on the side toward the forest, for many Indians lurked there with fire-arrows. And in a few years more, men built cabins on the south side of The Street.

Up and down The Street walked grave men in conical hats, who most of the time carried muskets or fowling pieces. And there were also their bonneted wives and sober children. In the evening these men with their wives and children would sit about gigantic hearths and read and speak. Very simple were the things of which they read and spoke, yet things which gave them courage and goodness and helped them by day to subdue the forest and till the fields. And the children would listen, and learn of the laws and deeds of old, and of that dear England which they had never seen, or could not remember.

There was war, and thereafter no more Indians troubled The Street. The men, busy with labor, waxed prosperous and as happy as they knew how to be. And the children grew up comfortably, and more families came from the Mother Land to dwell on The Street. And the children's children, and the newcomers' children, grew up. The town was now a city, and one by one the cabins gave place to houses; simple, beautiful houses of brick and wood, with stone steps and iron railings and fanlights over the doors.

No flimsy creations were these houses, for they were made to serve many a generation. Within there were carven mantels and graceful stairs, and sensible, pleasing furniture, china, and silver, brought from the Mother Land.

So The Street drank in the dreams of a young people, and rejoiced as its dwellers became more graceful and happy. Where once had been only strength and honor, taste and learning now abode as well. Books and paintings and music came to the houses, and the young men went to the university which rose above the plain to the north. In the place of conical hats and muskets there were three-cornered hats and small-swords, and lace and snowy periwigs. And there were cobblestones over which clattered many a blooded horse and rumbled many a gilded coach; and brick sidewalks with horse blocks and hitching-posts.

There were in that Street many trees; elms and oaks and maples of dignity; so that in the summer the scene was all soft verdure and twittering bird-song. And behind the houses were walled rose-gardens with hedged paths and sundials, where at evening the moon and stars would shine bewitchingly while fragrant blossoms glistened with dew.

So The Street dreamed on, past wars, calamities, and changes. Once most of the young men went away, and some never came back. That was when they furled the Old Flag and put up a new Banner of Stripes and Stars. But though men talked of great changes, The Street felt them not; for its folk were still the same, speaking of the old familiar things in the old familiar accents. And the trees still sheltered singing birds, and at evening the moon and stars looked down upon dewy blossoms in the walled rose-gardens.

In time there were no more swords, three-cornered hats, or periwigs in The Street. How strange seemed the denizens with their walking-sticks, tall beavers, and cropped heads! New sounds came from the distance – first strange puffings and shrieks from the river a mile away, and then, many years later, strange puffings and shrieks and rumblings from other directions. The air was not quite so pure as before, but the spirit of the place had not changed. The blood and soul of the people were as the blood and soul of their ancestors who had fashioned The Street. Nor did the spirit change when they tore open the earth to lay down strange pipes, or when they set up tall posts bearing weird wires. There was so much ancient lore in that Street, that the past could not easily be forgotten.

Then came days of evil, when many who had known The Street of old knew it no more; and many knew it, who had not known it before. And those who came were never as those who went away; for their accents were coarse and strident, and their mien and faces unpleasing. Their thoughts, too, fought with the wise, just spirit of The Street, so that The Street pined silently as its houses fell into decay, and its trees died one by one, and its rose-gardens grew rank with weeds and waste. But it felt a stir of pride one day when again marched forth young men, some of whom never came back. These young men were clad in blue.

With the years worse fortune came to The Street. Its trees were all gone now, and its rose-gardens were displaced by the backs of cheap, ugly new buildings on parallel streets. Yet the houses remained, despite the ravages of the years and the storms and worms, for they had been made to serve many a generation. New kinds of faces appeared in The Street; swarthy, sinister faces with furtive eyes and odd features, whose owners spoke unfamiliar words and placed signs in known and unknown characters upon most of the musty houses. Push-carts crowded the gutters. A sordid, undefinable stench settled over the place, and the ancient spirit slept.

Great excitement once came to The Street. War and revolution were raging across the seas; a dynasty had collapsed, and its degenerate subjects were flocking with dubious intent to the Western Land. Many of these took lodgings in the battered houses that had once known the songs of birds and the scent of roses. Then the Western Land itself awoke, and joined the

Mother Land in her titanic struggle for civilization. Over the
cities once more floated the Old Flag, companioned by the
New Flag and by a plainer yet glorious Tri-color. But not many
flags floated over The Street, for therein brooded only fear and
hatred and ignorance. Again young men went forth, but not
quite as did the young men of those other days. Something was
lacking. And the sons of those young men of other days, who
did indeed go forth in olive-drab with the true spirit of their
ancestors, went from distant places and knew not The Street
and its ancient spirit.

Over the seas there was a great victory, and in triumph most
of the young men returned. Those who had lacked something
lacked it no longer, yet did fear and hatred and ignorance still
brood over The Street; for many had stayed behind, and many
strangers had come from distant places to the ancient houses.
And the young men who had returned dwelt there no longer.
Swarthy and sinister were most of the strangers, yet among them
one might find a few faces like those who fashioned The Street
and molded its spirit. Like and yet unlike, for there was in the
eyes of all a weird, unhealthy glitter as of greed, ambition,
vindictiveness, or misguided zeal. Unrest and treason were
abroad amongst an evil few who plotted to strike the Western
Land its death-blow, that they might mount to power over its
ruins; even as assassins had mounted in that unhappy, frozen
land from whence most of them had come. And the heart of
that plotting was in The Street, whose crumbling houses teemed
with alien makers of discord and echoed with the plans and
speeches of those who yearned for the appointed day of blood,
flame, and crime.

Of the various odd assemblages in The Street, the law said
much but could prove little. With great diligence did men of
hidden badges linger and listen about such places as Petrovitch's
Bakery, the squalid Rifkin School of Modern Economics, the Circle
Social Club, and the Liberty Café. There congregated sinister men
in great numbers, yet always was their speech guarded or in a

foreign tongue. And still the old houses stood, with their forgotten lore of nobler, departed centuries; of sturdy colonial tenants and dewy rose-gardens in the moonlight. Sometimes a lone poet or traveler would come to view them, and would try to picture them in their vanished glory; yet of such travelers and poets there were not many.

The rumor now spread widely that these houses contained the leaders of a vast band of terrorists, who on a designated day were to launch an orgy of slaughter for the extermination of America and of all the fine old traditions which The Street had loved. Handbills and papers fluttered about filthy gutters; handbills and papers printed in many tongues and in many characters, yet all bearing messages of crime and rebellion. In these writings the people were urged to tear down the laws and virtues that our fathers had exalted; to stamp out the soul of the old America – the soul that was bequeathed through a thousand and a half years of Anglo-Saxon freedom, justice, and moderation. It was said that the swart men who dwelt in The Street and congregated in its rotting edifices were the brains of a hideous revolution; that at their word of command many millions of brainless, besotted beasts would stretch forth their noisome talons from the slums of a thousand cities, burning, slaying, and destroying till the land of our fathers should be no more. All this was said and repeated, and many looked forward in dread to the fourth day of July, about which the strange writings hinted much; yet could nothing be found to place the guilt. None could tell just whose arrest might cut off the damnable plotting at its source. Many times came bands of blue-coated police to search the shaky houses, though at last they ceased to come; for they too had grown tired of law and order, and had abandoned all the city to its fate. Then men in olive-drab came, bearing muskets; till it seemed as if in its sad sleep The Street must have some haunting dreams of those other days, when musket-bearing men in conical hats walked along it from the woodland spring to the cluster of houses by the beach. Yet could no act be performed to check the impending cataclysm; for the swart, sinister men were old in cunning.

So The Street slept uneasily on, till one night there gathered in Petrovitch's Bakery and the Rifkin School of Modern Economics, and the Circle Social Club, and Liberty Café, and in other places as well, vast hordes of men whose eyes were big with horrible triumph and expectation. Over hidden wires strange messages traveled, and much was said of still stranger messages yet to travel; but most of this was not guessed till afterward, when the Western Land was safe from the peril. The men in olive-drab could not tell what was happening, or what they ought to do; for the swart, sinister men were skilled in subtlety and concealment.

And yet the men in olive-drab will always remember that night, and will speak of The Street as they tell of it to their grandchildren; for many of them were sent there toward morning on a mission unlike that which they had expected. It was known that this nest of anarchy was old, and that the houses were tottering from the ravages of the years and the storms and the worms; yet was the happening of that summer night a surprise because of its very queer uniformity. It was, indeed, an exceedingly singular happening; though after all a simple one. For without warning, in one of the small hours beyond midnight, all the ravages of the years and the storms and the worms came to a tremendous climax; and after the crash there was nothing left standing in The Street save two ancient chimneys and part of a stout brick wall. Nor did anything that had been alive come alive from the ruins.

A poet and a traveler, who came with the mighty crowd that sought the scene, tell odd stories. The poet says that all through the hours before dawn he beheld sordid ruins but indistinctly in the glare of the arc-lights; that there loomed above the wreckage another picture wherein he could descry moonlight and fair houses and elms and oaks and maples of dignity. And the traveler declares that instead of the place's wonted stench there lingered a delicate fragrance as of roses in full bloom. But are not the dreams of poets and the tales of travelers notoriously false?

There be those who say that things and places have souls, and there be those who say they have not; I dare not say, myself, but I have told you of The Street.

THE PICTURE
IN THE HOUSE

Searchers after horror haunt strange, far places. For them are the catacombs of Ptolemais, and the carven mausolea of the nightmare countries. They climb to the moonlit towers of ruined Rhine castles, and falter down black cobwebbed steps beneath the scattered stones of forgotten cities in Asia. The haunted wood and the desolate mountain are their shrines, and they linger around the sinister monoliths on uninhabited islands. But the true epicure in the terrible, to whom a new thrill of unutterable ghastliness is the chief end and justification of existence, esteems most of all the ancient, lonely farmhouses of backwoods New England; for there the dark elements of strength, solitude, grotesqueness, and ignorance combine to form the perfection of the hideous.

Most horrible of all sights are the little unpainted wooden houses remote from traveled ways, usually squatted upon some damp, grassy slope or leaning against some gigantic outcropping of rock. Two hundred years and more they have leaned or squatted there, while the vines have crawled and the trees have swelled and spread. They are almost hidden now in lawless luxuriances of green and guardian shrouds of shadow; but the small-paned windows still stare shockingly, as if blinking through a lethal stupor which wards off madness by dulling the memory of unutterable things.

In such houses have dwelt generations of strange people, whose like the world has never seen. Seized with a gloomy and fanatical belief which exiled them from their kind, their ancestors sought the wilderness for freedom. There the scions of a conquering race indeed flourished free from the restrictions of their fellows, but cowered in an appalling slavery to the dismal phantasms of their own minds. Divorced from the enlightenment of civilization, the strength of these Puritans turned into singular channels; and in their isolation, morbid self-repression, and struggle for life with relentless Nature, there came to them dark furtive traits from the prehistoric depths of their cold Northern heritage. By necessity practical and by philosophy stern, these folk were not beautiful in their sins. Erring as all mortals must, they were forced by their rigid code to seek concealment above all else; so that they came to use less and less taste in what they concealed. Only the silent, sleepy, staring houses in the backwoods can tell all that has lain hidden since the early days; and they are not communicative, being loath to shake off the drowsiness which helps them forget. Sometimes one feels that it would be merciful to tear down these houses, for they must often dream.

It was to a time-battered edifice of this description that I was driven one afternoon in November, 1896, by a rain of such chilling copiousness that any shelter was preferable to exposure. I had been traveling for some time amongst the people of the Miskatonic Valley in quest of certain genealogical data; and from the remote, devious, and problematical nature of my course, had deemed it convenient to employ a bicycle despite the lateness of the season. Now I found myself upon an apparently abandoned road which I had chosen as the shortest cut to Arkham; overtaken by the storm at a point far from any town, and confronted with no refuge save the antique and repellent wooden building which blinked with bleared windows from between two huge leafless elms near the foot of a rocky hill. Distant though it was from the remnant of a road, the house none the less impressed me unfavorably the very moment I espied it. Honest, wholesome structures do not stare at travelers so slyly and hauntingly, and in my genealogical researches I had encountered legends of a century before which biassed me against places of this kind. Yet the force of the elements was such as to overcome my scruples, and I did not hesitate to wheel my machine up the weedy rise to the closed door which seemed at once so suggestive and secretive.

I had somehow taken it for granted that the house was abandoned, yet as I approached it I was not so sure; for though the walks were indeed overgrown with weeds, they seemed to retain their nature a little too well to argue complete desertion. Therefore instead of trying the door I knocked, feeling as I did so a trepidation I could scarcely explain. As I waited on the rough, mossy rock which served as a doorstep, I glanced at the neighboring windows and the panes of the transom above me, and noticed that although old, rattling, and almost opaque with dirt, they were not broken. The building, then, must still be inhabited, despite its isolation and general neglect. However, my rapping evoked no response, so after repeating the summons I tried the rusty latch and found the door unfastened. Inside was a little vestibule with walls from which the plaster was falling, and through the doorway came a faint but peculiarly hateful odor. I entered, carrying my bicycle, and closed the door behind me. Ahead rose a narrow staircase, flanked by a small door probably leading to the cellar, while to the left and right were closed doors leading to rooms on the ground floor.

Leaning my cycle against the wall I opened the door at the left, and crossed into a small low-ceiled chamber but dimly lighted by its two dusty windows and furnished in the barest and most primitive possible way. It appeared to be a kind of sitting-room, for it had a table and several chairs, and an immense fireplace above which ticked an antique clock on a mantel. Books and papers were very few, and in the prevailing gloom I could not readily discern the titles. What interested me was the uniform air of archaism as displayed in every visible detail. Most of the houses in this region I had found rich in relics of the past, but here the antiquity was curiously complete; for in all the room I could not discover a single article of definitely post-revolutionary date. Had the furnishings been less humble, the place would have been a collector's paradise.

As I surveyed this quaint apartment, I felt an increase in that aversion first excited by the bleak exterior of the house. Just what it was that I feared or loathed, I could by no means define; but something in the whole atmosphere seemed redolent of unhallowed age, of unpleasant crudeness, and of secrets which should be forgotten. I felt disinclined to sit down, and wandered about examining the various articles which I had noticed. The first object of my curiosity was a book of medium size lying upon the table and presenting such an antediluvian aspect that I marveled at beholding it outside a museum or library. It was bound in leather with metal fittings, and was in an excellent state of preservation; being altogether an unusual sort of volume to encounter in an abode so lowly. When I opened it to the title page my wonder grew even greater, for it proved to be nothing less rare than Pigafetta's account of the Congo region, written in Latin from the notes of the sailor Lopez and printed at Frankfort in 1598. I had often heard of this work, with its curious illustrations by the brothers De Bry, hence for a moment forgot my uneasiness in my desire to turn the pages before me. The engravings were indeed interesting, drawn wholly from imagination and careless descriptions, and represented negroes with white skins and Caucasian features; nor would I soon have closed the book had not an exceedingly trivial circumstance upset my tired nerves and revived my sensation of disquiet. What annoyed me was merely the persistent way in which the volume tended to fall open of itself at Plate XII, which represented in gruesome detail a butcher's shop of the cannibal Anziques. I experienced some shame at my susceptibility to so slight a thing, but the drawing nevertheless disturbed me, especially in connexion with some adjacent passages descriptive of Anzique gastronomy.

I had turned to a neighboring shelf and was examining its meager literary contents – an eighteenth-century Bible, a *Pilgrim's Progress* of like period, illustrated with grotesque woodcuts and printed by the almanack-maker Isaiah Thomas, the rotting bulk of Cotton Mather's *Magnalia Christi Americana,* and a few other books of evidently equal age – when my attention was aroused by the unmistakable sound of walking in the room overhead. At first astonished and startled, considering the lack of response to my recent knocking at the door, I immediately afterward concluded that the walker had just awakened from a sound sleep; and listened with less surprise as the footsteps sounded on the creaking stairs. The tread was heavy, yet seemed to contain a curious quality of cautiousness; a quality which I disliked the more because the tread was heavy. When I had entered the room I had shut the door behind me. Now, after a moment of silence during which the walker may have been inspecting my bicycle in the hall, I heard a fumbling at the latch and saw the paneled portal swing open again.

In the doorway stood a person of such singular appearance that I should have exclaimed aloud but for the restraints of good breeding. Old, white-bearded, and ragged, my host possessed a countenance and physique which inspired equal wonder and respect. His height could not have been less than six feet, and despite a general air of age and poverty he was stout and powerful in proportion. His face, almost hidden by a long beard which grew high on the cheeks, seemed abnormally ruddy and less wrinkled than one might expect; while over a high forehead fell a shock of white hair little thinned by the years. His blue eyes, though a trifle bloodshot, seemed inexplicably keen and burning. But for his horrible unkemptness the man would have been as distinguished-looking as he was impressive. This unkemptness, however, made him offensive despite his face and figure. Of what his clothing consisted I could hardly tell, for it seemed to me no more than a mass of tatters surmounting a pair of high, heavy boots; and his lack of cleanliness surpassed description.

The appearance of this man, and the instinctive fear he inspired, prepared me for something like enmity; so that I almost shuddered through surprise and a sense of uncanny incongruity when he motioned me to a chair and addressed me in a thin, weak voice full of fawning respect and ingratiating hospitality. His speech was very curious, an extreme form of Yankee dialect I had thought long extinct; and I studied it closely as he sat down opposite me for conversation.

"Ketched in the rain, be ye?" he greeted. "Glad ye was nigh the haouse en' hed the sense ta come right in. I calc'late I was asleep, else I'd a heerd ye – I ain't as young as I uster be, an' I need a paowerful sight o' naps naowadays. Trav'lin' fur? I hain't seed many folks 'long this rud sence they tuk off the Arkham stage."

I replied that I was going to Arkham, and apologized for my rude entry into his domicile, whereupon he continued.

"Glad ta see ye, young Sir – new faces is scurce arount here, an' I hain't got much ta cheer me up these days. Guess yew hail from Bosting, don't ye? I never ben thar, but I kin tell a taown man when I see 'im – we hed one fer deestrick schoolmaster in 'eighty-four, but he quit suddent an' no one never heerd on 'im sence—" Here the old man lapsed into a kind of chuckle, and made no explanation when I questioned him. He seemed to be in an aboundingly good humor, yet to possess those eccentricities which one might guess from his grooming. For some time he rambled on with an almost feverish geniality, when it struck me to ask him how he came by so rare a book as Pigafetta's *Regnum Congo*. The effect of this volume had not left me, and I felt a certain hesitancy in speaking of it; but curiosity overmastered all the vague fears which had steadily accumulated since my first glimpse of the house. To my relief, the question did not seem an awkward one; for the old man answered freely and volubly.

"Oh, thet Afriky book? Cap'n Ebenezer Holt traded me thet in 'sixty-eight – him as was kilt in the war." Something about the name of Ebenezer Holt caused me to look up sharply. I had encountered it in my genealogical work, but not in any record since the Revolution. I wondered if my host could help me in the task at which I was laboring, and resolved to ask him about it later on. He continued.

"Ebenezer was on a Salem merchantman for years, an' picked up a sight o' queer stuff in every port. He got this in London, I guess – he uster like ter buy things at the shops. I was up ta his haouse onct, on the hill, tradin' hosses, when I see this book. I relished the picters, so he give it in on a swap. 'Tis a queer book – here, leave me git on my spectacles—" The old man fumbled among his rags, producing a pair of dirty and amazingly antique glasses with small octagonal lenses and steel bows. Donning these, he reached for the volume on the table and turned the pages lovingly.

"Ebenezer cud read a leetle o' this – 'tis Latin – but I can't. I hed two er three schoolmasters read me a bit, and Passon Clark, him they say got draownded in the pond – kin yew make anything outen it?" I told him that I could, and translated for his benefit a paragraph near the beginning. If I erred, he was not scholar enough to correct me; for he seemed childishly pleased at my English version. His proximity was becoming rather obnoxious, yet I saw no way to escape without offending him. I was amused at the childish fondness of this ignorant old man for the pictures in a book he could not read, and wondered how much better he could read the few books in English which adorned the room. This revelation of simplicity removed much of the ill-defined apprehension I had felt, and I smiled as my host rambled on:

"Queer haow picters kin set a body thinkin'. Take this un here near the front. Hev yew ever seed trees like thet, with big leaves a-floppin' over an' daown? And them men – them can't be niggers – they dew beat all. Kinder like Injuns, I guess, even ef they be in Afriky. Some o' these here critters looks like monkeys, or half monkeys an' half men, but I never heerd o' nothing like this un." Here he pointed to a fabulous creature of the artist, which one might describe as a sort of dragon with the head of an alligator.

"But naow I'll shew ye the best un – over here nigh the

middle—" The old man's speech grew a trifle thicker and his
eyes assumed a brighter glow; but his fumbling hands, though
seemingly clumsier than before, were entirely adequate to their
mission. The book fell open, almost of its own accord and as if
from frequent consultation at this place, to the repellent twelfth
plate shewing a butcher's shop amongst the Anzique cannibals.
My sense of restlessness returned, though I did not exhibit it.
The especially bizarre thing was that the artist had made his
Africans look like white men - the limbs and quarters hanging
about the walls of the shop were ghastly, while the butcher with
his axe was hideously incongruous. But my host seemed to relish
the view as much as I disliked it.

"What d'ye think o' this - ain't never see the like hereabouts,
eh? When I see this I telled Eb Holt, 'That's suthin' ta stir ye up
an' make yer blood tickle!' When I read in Scripter about slayin'
- like them Midianites was slew - I kinder think things, but I
ain't got no picter of it. Here a body kin see all they is to it - I
s'pose 'tis sinful, but ain't we all born an' livin' in sin? - Thet
feller bein' chopped up gives me a tickle every time I look at
'im - I hev ta keep lookin' at 'im - see whar the butcher cut off
his feet? Thar's his head on thet bench, with one arm side of it,
an' t'other arm's on the graound side o' the meat block."

As the man mumbled on in his shocking ecstasy the expression on his hairy, spectacled face became indescribable, but his
voice sank rather than mounted. My own sensations can scarcely
be recorded. All the terror I had dimly felt before rushed upon
me actively and vividly, and I knew that I loathed the ancient
and abhorrent creature so near me with an infinite intensity. His
madness, or at least his partial perversion, seemed beyond dispute.
He was almost whispering now, with a huskiness more terrible
than a scream, and I trembled as I listened.

"As I says, 'tis queer haow picters sets ye thinkin'. D'ye know,
young Sir, I'm right sot on this un here. Arter I got the book off
Eb I uster look at it a lot, especial when I'd heerd Passon Clark
rant o' Sundays in his big wig. Onct I tried suthin' funny - here,

young Sir, don't git skeert – all I done was ter look at the picter afore I kilt the sheep for market – killin' sheep was kinder more fun arter lookin' at it—"The tone of the old man now sank very low, sometimes becoming so faint that his words were hardly audible. I listened to the rain, and to the rattling of the bleared, small-paned windows, and marked a rumbling of approaching thunder quite unusual for the season. Once a terrific flash and peal shook the frail house to its foundations, but the whisperer seemed not to notice it.

"Killin' sheep was kinder more fun – but d'ye know, 'twan't quite *satisfyin'*. Queer haow a *cravin'* gits a holt on ye – As ye love the Almighty, young man, don't tell nobody, but I swar ter Gawd thet picter begun ta make me *hungry fer victuals I couldn't raise nor buy* – here, set still, what's ailin' ye? – I didn't do nothin', only I wondered haow 'twud be ef I *did* – They say meat makes blood an' flesh, an' gives ye new life, so I wondered ef 'twudn't make a man live longer an' longer ef 'twas *more the same*—" But the whisperer never continued. The interruption was not produced by my fright, nor by the rapidly increasing storm amidst whose fury I was presently to open my eyes on a smoky solitude of blackened ruins. It was produced by a very simple though somewhat unusual happening.

The open book lay flat between us, with the picture staring repulsively upward. As the old man whispered the words *"more the same"* a tiny spattering impact was heard, and something shewed on the yellowed paper of the upturned volume. I thought of the rain and of a leaky roof, but rain is not red. On the butcher's shop of the Anzique cannibals a small red spattering glistened picturesquely, lending vividness to the horror of the engraving. The old man saw it, and stopped whispering even before my expression of horror made it necessary; saw it and glanced quickly toward the floor of the room he had left an hour before. I followed his glance, and beheld just above us on the loose plaster of the ancient ceiling a large irregular spot of wet crimson which seemed to spread even as I viewed it. I did not shriek or move, but merely shut my eyes. A moment later came the titanic thunderbolt of thunderbolts; blasting that accursed house of unutterable secrets and bringing the oblivion which alone saved my mind.

THE TREE

"Fata viam invenient."

On a verdant slope of Mount Maenalus, in Arcadia, there stands an olive grove about the ruins of a villa. Close by is a tomb, once beautiful with the sublimest sculptures, but now fallen into as great decay as the house. At one end of that tomb, its curious roots displacing the time-stained blocks of Pentelic marble, grows an unnaturally large olive tree of oddly repellent shape; so like to some grotesque man, or death-distorted body of a man, that the country folk fear to pass it at night when the moon shines faintly through the crooked boughs. Mount Maenalus is a chosen haunt of dreaded Pan, whose queer companions are many, and simple swains believe that the tree must have some hideous kinship to these weird Panisci; but an old bee-keeper who lives in the neighboring cottage told me a different story.

Many years ago, when the hillside villa was new and resplendent, there dwelt within it the two sculptors Kalos and Musides. From Lydia to Neapolis the beauty of their work was praised, and none dared say that the one excelled the other in skill. The Hermes of Kalos stood in a marble shrine in Corinth, and the Pallas of Musides surmounted a pillar in Athens, near the Parthenon. All men paid homage to Kalos and Musides, and marveled that no shadow of artistic jealousy cooled the warmth of their brotherly friendship.

But though Kalos and Musides dwelt in unbroken harmony, their natures were not alike. Whilst Musides reveled by night amidst the urban gaieties of Tegea, Kalos would remain at home; stealing away from the sight of his slaves into the cool recesses of the olive grove. There he would meditate upon the visions that filled his mind, and there devise the forms of beauty which later became immortal in breathing marble. Idle folk, indeed, said that Kalos conversed with the spirits of the grove, and that his statues were but images of the fauns and dryads he met there – for he patterned his work after no living model.

So famous were Kalos and Musides, that none wondered when the Tyrant of Syracuse sent to them deputies to speak of the costly statue of Tyché which he had planned for his city. Of great size and cunning workmanship must the statue be, for it was to form a wonder of nations and a goal of travelers. Exalted beyond thought would be he whose work should gain acceptance, and for this honor Kalos and Musides were invited to compete. Their brotherly love was well known, and the crafty Tyrant surmised that each, instead of concealing his work from the other, would offer aid and advice; this charity producing two images of unheard-of beauty, the lovelier of which would eclipse even the dreams of poets.

With joy the sculptors hailed the Tyrant's offer, so that in the days that followed their slaves heard the ceaseless blows of chisels. Not from each other did Kalos and Musides conceal their work, but the sight was for them alone. Saving theirs, no eyes beheld the two divine figures released by skillful blows from the rough blocks that had imprisoned them since the world began.

At night, as of yore, Musides sought the banquet halls of Tegea whilst Kalos wandered alone in the olive grove. But as time passed, men observed a want of gaiety in the once sparkling Musides. It was strange, they said amongst themselves, that depression should thus seize one with so great a chance to win art's loftiest reward. Many months passed, yet in the sour face of Musides came nothing of the sharp expectancy which the situation should arouse.

Then one day Musides spoke of the illness of Kalos, after which none marveled again at his sadness, since the sculptors' attachment was known to be deep and sacred. Subsequently many went to visit Kalos, and indeed noticed the pallor of his face; but there was about him a happy serenity which made his glance more magical than the glance of Musides – who was clearly distracted with anxiety, and who pushed aside all the slaves in his eagerness to feed and wait upon his friend with his own hands. Hidden behind heavy curtains stood the two unfinished figures of Tyché, little touched of late by the sick man and his faithful attendant.

As Kalos grew inexplicably weaker and weaker despite the ministrations of puzzled physicians and of his assiduous friend, he desired to be carried often to the grove which he so loved. There he would ask to be left alone, as if wishing to speak with unseen things. Musides ever granted his requests, though his eyes filled with visible tears at the thought that Kalos should care more for the fauns and the dryads than for him. At last the end drew near, and Kalos discoursed of things beyond this life. Musides, weeping, promised him a sepulcher more lovely than the tomb of Mausolus; but Kalos bade him speak no more of marble glories. Only one wish now haunted the mind of the dying man; that twigs from certain olive trees in the grove be buried by his resting-place – close to his head. And one night, sitting alone in the darkness of the olive grove, Kalos died.

Beautiful beyond words was the marble sepulcher which stricken Musides carved for his beloved friend. None but Kalos himself could have fashioned such bas-reliefs, wherein were displayed all the splendors of Elysium. Nor did Musides fail to bury close to Kalos' head the olive twigs from the grove.

As the first violence of Musides' grief gave place to resignation, he labored with diligence upon his figure of Tyché. All honor was now his, since the Tyrant of Syracuse would have the work of none save him or Kalos. His task proved a vent for his emotion, and he toiled more steadily each day, shunning the gaieties he once had relished. Meanwhile his evenings were spent beside the tomb of his friend, where a young olive tree had sprung up near the sleeper's head. So swift was the growth of this tree, and so strange was its form, that all who beheld it exclaimed in surprise; and Musides seemed at once fascinated and repelled.

Three years after the death of Kalos, Musides despatched a

messenger to the Tyrant, and it was whispered in the agora at Tegea that the mighty statue was finished. By this time the tree by the tomb had attained amazing proportions, exceeding all other trees of its kind, and sending out a singularly heavy branch above the apartment in which Musides labored. As many visitors came to view the prodigious tree, as to admire the art of the sculptor, so that Musides was seldom alone. But he did not mind his multitude of guests; indeed, he seemed to dread being alone now that his absorbing work was done. The bleak mountain wind, sighing through the olive grove and the tomb-tree, had an uncanny way of forming vaguely articulate sounds.

The sky was dark on the evening that the Tyrant's emissaries came to Tegea. It was definitely known that they had come to bear away the great image of Tyché and bring eternal honor to Musides, so their reception by the proxenoi was of great warmth. As the night wore on, a violent storm of wind broke over the crest of Maenalus, and the men from far Syracuse were glad that they rested snugly in the town. They talked of their illustrious Tyrant, and of the splendor of his capital; and exulted in the glory of the statue which Musides had wrought for him. And then the men of Tegea spoke of the goodness of Musides, and of his heavy grief for his friend; and how not even the coming laurels of art could console him in the absence of Kalos, who might have worn those laurels instead. Of the tree which grew by the tomb, near the head of Kalos, they also spoke. The wind shrieked more horribly, and both the Syracusans and the Arcadians prayed to Aiolos.

In the sunshine of the morning the proxenoi led the Tyrant's messengers up the slope to the abode of the sculptor, but the night-wind had done strange things. Slaves' cries ascended from a scene of desolation, and no more amidst the olive grove rose the gleaming colonnades of that vast hall wherein Musides had dreamed and toiled. Lone and shaken mourned the humble courts and the lower walls, for upon the sumptuous greater peristyle had fallen squarely the heavy overhanging bough of the strange new tree, reducing the stately poem in marble with odd completeness to a mound of unsightly ruins. Strangers and Tegeans stood aghast, looking from the wreckage to the great, sinister tree whose aspect was so weirdly human and whose roots reached so queerly into the sculptured sepulcher of Kalos. And their fear and dismay increased when they searched the fallen apartment; for of the gentle Musides, and of the marvelously fashioned image of Tyché, no trace could be discovered. Amidst such stupendous ruin only chaos dwelt, and the representatives of two cities left disappointed; Syracusans that they had no statue to bear home, Tegeans that they had no artist to crown. However, the Syracusans obtained after a while a very splendid statue in Athens, and the Tegeans consoled themselves by erecting in the agora a marble temple commemorating the gifts, virtues, and brotherly piety of Musides.

But the olive grove still stands, as does the tree growing out of the tomb of Kalos, and the old bee-keeper told me that sometimes the boughs whisper to one another in the night-wind, saying over and over again, *"Oida! Oida! – I know! I know!"*

THE MUSIC OF ERICH ZANN

I have examined maps of the city with the greatest care, yet have never again found the Rue d'Auseil. These maps have not been modern maps alone, for I know that names change. I have, on the contrary, delved deeply into all the antiquities of the place; and have personally explored every region, of whatever name, which could possibly answer to the street I knew as the Rue d'Auseil. But despite all I have done it remains an humiliating fact that I cannot find the house, the street, or even the locality, where, during the last months of my impoverished life as a student of metaphysics at the university, I heard the music of Erich Zann.

That my memory is broken, I do not wonder; for my health, physical and mental, was gravely disturbed throughout the period of my residence in the Rue d'Auseil, and I recall that I took none of my few acquaintances there. But that I cannot find the place again is both singular and perplexing; for it was within a half-hour's walk of the university and was distinguished by peculiarities which could hardly be forgotten by anyone who had been there. I have never met a person who has seen the Rue d'Auseil.

The Rue d'Auseil lay across a dark river bordered by precipitous brick blear-windowed warehouses and spanned by a ponderous bridge of dark stone. It was always shadowy along that river, as if the smoke of neighboring factories shut out the sun perpetually. The river was also odorous with evil stenches which I have never smelled elsewhere, and which may some day help me to find it, since I should recognize them at once. Beyond the bridge were narrow cobbled streets with rails; and then came the ascent, at first gradual, but incredibly steep as the Rue d'Auseil was reached.

I have never seen another street as narrow and steep as the

Rue d'Auseil. It was almost a cliff, closed to all vehicles, consisting in several places of flights of steps, and ending at the top in a lofty ivied wall. Its paving was irregular, sometimes stone slabs, sometimes cobblestones, and sometimes bare earth with struggling greenish-gray vegetation. The houses were tall, peaked-roofed, incredibly old, and crazily leaning backward, forward, and sidewise. Occasionally an opposite pair, both leaning forward, almost met across the street like an arch; and certainly they kept most of the light from the ground below. There were a few overhead bridges from house to house across the street.

The inhabitants of that street impressed me peculiarly. At first I thought it was because they were all silent and reticent; but later decided it was because they were all very old. I do not know how I came to live on such a street, but I was not myself when I moved there. I had been living in many poor places, always evicted for want of money; until at last I came upon that tottering house in the Rue d'Auseil, kept by the paralytic Blandot. It was the third house from the top of the street, and by far the tallest of them all.

My room was on the fifth story; the only inhabited room there, since the house was almost empty. On the night I arrived I heard strange music from the peaked garret overhead, and the next day asked old Blandot about it. He told me it was an old German viol-player, a strange dumb man who signed his name as Erich Zann, and who played evenings in a cheap theater orchestra; adding that Zann's desire to play in the night after his return from the theater was the reason he had chosen this lofty and isolated garret room, whose single gable window was the only point on the street from which one could look over the terminating wall at the declivity and panorama beyond.

Thereafter I heard Zann every night, and although he kept me awake, I was haunted by the weirdness of his music. Knowing little of the art myself, I was yet certain that none of his harmonies had any relation to music I had heard before; and concluded that he was a composer of highly original genius. The longer I listened, the more I was fascinated, until after a week I resolved to make the old man's acquaintance.

One night, as he was returning from his work, I intercepted Zann in the hallway and told him that I would like to know him and be with him when he played. He was a small, lean, bent person, with shabby clothes, blue eyes, grotesque, satyr-like face, and nearly bald head; and at my first words seemed both angered and frightened. My obvious friendliness, however, finally melted him; and he grudgingly motioned to me to follow him up the dark, creaking, and rickety attic stairs. His room, one of only two in the steeply pitched garret, was on the west side, toward the high wall that formed the upper end of the street. Its size was very great, and seemed the greater because of its extraordinary bareness and neglect. Of furniture there was only a narrow iron bedstead, a dingy washstand, a small table, a large bookcase, an iron music-rack, and three old-fashioned chairs. Sheets of music were piled in disorder about the floor. The walls were of bare boards, and had probably never known plaster; whilst the abundance of dust and cobwebs made the place seem more deserted than inhabited. Evidently Erich Zann's world of beauty lay in some far cosmos of the imagination.

Motioning me to sit down, the dumb man closed the door, turned the large wooden bolt, and lighted a candle to augment the one he had brought with him. He now removed his viol from its moth-eaten covering, and taking it, seated himself in the least uncomfortable of the chairs. He did not employ the music-rack, but offering no choice and playing from memory, enchanted me for over an hour with strains I had never heard before; strains which must have been of his own devising. To describe their exact nature is impossible for one unversed in music. They were a kind of fugue, with recurrent passages of the most captivating quality, but to me were notable for the absence of any of the weird notes I had overheard from my room below on other occasions.

Those haunting notes I had remembered, and had often hummed and whistled inaccurately to myself; so when the player at length laid down his bow I asked him if he would render some of them. As I began my request the wrinkled satyr-like face lost the bored placidity it had possessed during the playing, and seemed to shew the same curious mixture of anger and fright which I had noticed when first I accosted the old man. For a moment I was inclined to use persuasion, regarding rather lightly the whims of senility; and even tried to awaken my host's weirder mood by whistling a few of the strains to which I had listened the night before. But I did not pursue this course for more than a moment; for when the dumb musician recognized the whistled air his face grew suddenly distorted with an expression wholly beyond analysis, and his long, cold, bony right hand reached out to stop my mouth and silence the crude imitation. As he did this he further demonstrated his eccentricity by casting a startled glance toward the lone curtained window, as if fearful of some intruder – a glance doubly absurd, since the garret stood high and inaccessible above all the adjacent roofs, this window being the only point on the steep street, as the concierge had told me, from which one could see over the wall at the summit.

The old man's glance brought Blandot's remark to my mind, and with a certain capriciousness I felt a wish to look out over the wide and dizzying panorama of moonlit roofs and city lights beyond the hill-top, which of all the dwellers in the Rue d'Auseil only this crabbed musician could see. I moved toward the window and would have drawn aside the nondescript curtains, when with a frightened rage even greater than before the dumb lodger was upon me again; this time motioning with his head toward the door as he nervously strove to drag me thither with both hands. Now thoroughly disgusted with my host, I ordered him to release me, and told him I would go at once. His clutch relaxed, and as he saw my disgust and offense his own anger seemed to subside. He tightened his relaxing grip, but this time in a friendly manner; forcing me into a chair, then with an appearance of wistfulness crossing to the littered table, where he wrote many words with a pencil in the labored French of a foreigner.

The note which he finally handed me was an appeal for tolerance and forgiveness. Zann said that he was old, lonely, and afflicted with strange fears and nervous disorders connected with his music and with other things. He had enjoyed my listening to his music, and wished I would come again and not mind his eccentricities. But he could not play to another his weird harmonies, and could not bear hearing them from another; nor could he bear having anything in his room touched by another. He had not known until our hallway conversation that I could overhear his playing in my room, and now asked me if I would arrange with Blandot to take a lower room where I could not hear him in the night. He would, he wrote, defray the difference in rent.

As I sat deciphering the execrable French I felt more lenient toward the old man. He was a victim of physical and nervous suffering, as was I; and my metaphysical studies had taught me kindness. In the silence there came a slight sound from the window – the shutter must have rattled in the night-wind – and for some reason I started almost as violently as did Erich Zann. So when I had finished reading I shook my host by the hand, and departed as a friend. The next day Blandot gave me a more expensive room on the third floor, between the apartments of an aged money-lender and the room of a respectable upholsterer. There was no one on the fourth floor.

It was not long before I found that Zann's eagerness for my company was not as great as it had seemed while he was persuading me to move down from the fifth story. He did not ask me to call on him, and when I did call he appeared uneasy and played listlessly. This was always at night – in the day he slept and would admit no one. My liking for him did not grow, though the attic room and the weird music seemed to hold an odd fascination for me. I had a curious desire to look out of that window, over the wall and down the unseen slope at the glittering roofs and spires which must lie outspread there. Once I went up to the garret during theater hours, when Zann was away, but the door was locked.

What I did succeed in doing was to overhear the nocturnal playing of the dumb old man. At first I would tiptoe up to my old fifth floor, then I grew bold enough to climb the last creaking staircase to the peaked garret. There in the narrow hall, outside the bolted door with the covered keyhole, I often heard sounds which filled me with an indefinable dread – the dread of vague wonder and brooding mystery. It was not that the sounds were hideous, for they were not; but that they held vibrations suggesting nothing on this globe of earth, and that at certain intervals they assumed a symphonic quality which I could hardly conceive as produced by one player. Certainly, Erich Zann was a genius of wild power. As the weeks passed, the playing grew wilder, whilst the old musician acquired an increasing haggard- ness and furtiveness pitiful to behold. He now refused to admit me at any time, and shunned me whenever we met on the stairs.

Then one night as I listened at the door I heard the shrieking viol swell into a chaotic babel of sound; a pandemonium which would have led me to doubt my own shaking sanity had there not come from behind that barred portal a piteous proof that the horror was real – the awful, inarticulate cry which only a mute can utter, and which rises only in moments of the most terrible fear or anguish. I knocked repeatedly at the door, but received no response. Afterward I waited in the black hallway, shivering with cold and fear, till I heard the poor musician's feeble effort to rise from the floor by the aid of a chair. Believing him just conscious after a fainting fit, I renewed my rapping, at the same time calling out my name reassuringly. I heard Zann stumble to the window and close both shutter and sash, then stumble to the door, which he falteringly unfastened to admit me. This time his delight at having me present was real; for his distorted face gleamed with relief while he clutched at my coat as a child clutches at its mother's skirts.

Shaking pathetically, the old man forced me into a chair whilst he sank into another, beside which his viol and bow lay carelessly on the floor. He sat for some time inactive, nodding oddly, but having a paradoxical suggestion of intense and frightened listening. Subsequently he seemed to be satisfied, and crossing to a chair by the table wrote a brief note, handed it to me, and returned to the table, where he began to write rapidly and incessantly. The note implored me in the name of mercy, and for the sake of my own curiosity, to wait where I was while he prepared a full account in German of all the marvels and terrors which beset him. I waited, and the dumb man's pencil flew.

It was perhaps an hour later, while I still waited and while the old musician's feverishly written sheets still continued to pile up, that I saw Zann start as from the hint of a horrible shock. Unmistakably he was looking at the curtained window and listening shudderingly. Then I half fancied I heard a sound myself; though it was not a horrible sound, but rather an exquisitely low and infinitely distant musical note, suggesting a player in one of the neighboring houses, or in some abode beyond the lofty wall over which I had never been able to look. Upon Zann the effect was terrible, for dropping his pencil suddenly he rose, seized his viol, and commenced to rend the night with the wildest playing I had ever heard from his bow save when listening at the barred door.

It would be useless to describe the playing of Erich Zann on that dreadful night. It was more horrible than anything I had ever overheard, because I could now see the expression of his face, and could realize that this time the motive was stark fear. He was trying to make a noise; to ward something off or drown something out – what, I could not imagine, awesome though I felt it must be. The playing grew fantastic, delirious, and hysterical, yet kept to the last the qualities of supreme genius which I knew this strange old man possessed. I recognized the air – it was a wild Hungarian dance popular in the theaters, and I reflected for a moment that this was the first time I had ever heard Zann play the work of another composer.

Louder and louder, wilder and wilder, mounted the shrieking and whining of that desperate viol. The player was dripping with an uncanny perspiration and twisted like a monkey, always looking frantically at the curtained window. In his frenzied strains I could almost see shadowy satyrs and Bacchanals dancing and whirling insanely through seething abysses of clouds and smoke and lightning. And then I thought I heard a shriller, steadier note that was not from the viol; a calm, deliberate, purposeful, mocking note from far away in the west.

At this juncture the shutter began to rattle in a howling night-wind which had sprung up outside as if in answer to the mad playing within. Zann's screaming viol now outdid itself, emitting sounds I had never thought a viol could emit. The shutter rattled more loudly, unfastened, and commenced slamming against the window. Then the glass broke shiveringly under the persistent impacts, and the chill wind rushed in, making the candles sputter and rustling the sheets of paper on the table where Zann had begun to write out his horrible secret. I looked at Zann, and saw that he was past conscious observation. His blue eyes were bulging, glassy, and sightless, and the frantic playing had become a blind, mechanical, unrecognizable orgy that no pen could even suggest.

A sudden gust, stronger than the others, caught up the manuscript and bore it toward the window. I followed the flying sheets in desperation, but they were gone before I reached the demolished panes. Then I remembered my old wish to gaze from this window, the only window in the Rue d'Auseil from which one might see the slope beyond the wall, and the city outspread beneath. It was very dark, but the city's lights always burned, and I expected to see them there amidst the rain and wind. Yet when I looked from that highest of all gable windows, looked while the candles sputtered and the insane viol howled with the night-wind, I saw no city spread below, and no friendly lights gleaming from remembered streets, but only the blackness of space illimitable; unimagined space alive with motion and music, and having no semblance to anything on earth. And as I stood there looking in terror, the wind blew out both the candles in that ancient peaked garret, leaving me in savage and impenetrable darkness with chaos and pandemonium before me, and the daemon madness of that night-baying viol behind me.

I staggered back in the dark, without the means of striking a light, crashing against the table, overturning a chair, and finally groping my way to the place where the blackness screamed with shocking music. To save myself and Erich Zann I could at least try, whatever the powers opposed to me. Once I thought some chill thing brushed me, and I screamed, but my scream could not be heard above that hideous viol. Suddenly out of the blackness the madly sawing bow struck me, and I knew I was close to the player. I felt ahead, touched the back of Zann's chair, and then found and shook his shoulder in an effort to bring him to his senses.

He did not respond, and still the viol shrieked on without slackening. I moved my hand to his head, whose mechanical nodding I was able to stop, and shouted in his ear that we must both flee from the unknown things of the night. But he neither answered me nor abated the frenzy of his unutterable music, while all through the garret strange currents of wind seemed to dance in the darkness and babel. When my hand touched his ear I shuddered, though I knew not why – knew not why till I felt of the still face; the ice-cold, stiffened, unbreathing face whose glassy eyes bulged uselessly into the void. And then, by some miracle finding the door and the large wooden bolt, I plunged wildly away from that glassy-eyed thing in the dark, and from the ghoulish howling of that accursed viol whose fury increased even as I plunged.

Leaping, floating, flying down those endless stairs through the dark house; racing mindlessly out into the narrow, steep, and ancient street of steps and tottering houses; clattering down steps and over cobbles to the lower streets and the putrid canyon-walled river; panting across the great dark bridge to the broader, healthier streets and boulevards we know; all these are terrible impressions that linger with me. And I recall that there was no wind, and that the moon was out, and that all the lights of the city twinkled.

Despite my most careful searches and investigations, I have never since been able to find the Rue d'Auseil. But I am not wholly sorry; either for this or for the loss in undreamable abysses of the closely written sheets which alone could have explained the music of Erich Zann.

IN THE VAULT

DEDICATED TO C. W. SMITH,
FROM WHOSE SUGGESTION THE
CENTRAL SITUATION IS TAKEN

There is nothing more absurd, as I view it, than that conventional association of the homely and the wholesome which seems to pervade the psychology of the multitude. Mention a bucolic Yankee setting, a bungling and thick-fibered village undertaker, and a careless mishap in a tomb, and no average reader can be brought to expect more than a hearty albeit grotesque phase of comedy. God knows, though, that the prosy tale which George Birch's death permits me to tell has in it aspects beside which some of our darkest tragedies are light.

Birch acquired a limitation and changed his business in 1881, yet never discussed the case when he could avoid it. Neither did his old physician Dr. Davis, who died years ago. It was generally stated that the affliction and shock were results of an unlucky slip whereby Birch had locked himself for nine hours in the receiving tomb of Peck Valley Cemetery, escaping only by crude and disastrous mechanical means; but while this much was undoubtedly true, there were other and blacker things which the man used to whisper to me in his drunken delirium toward the last. He confided in me because I was his doctor, and because he probably felt the need of confiding in someone else after Davis died. He was a bachelor, wholly without relatives.

Birch, before 1881, had been the village undertaker of Peck Valley; and was a very calloused and primitive specimen even as such specimens go. The practices I heard attributed to him would be unbelievable today, at least in a city; and even Peck Valley would have shuddered a bit had it known the easy ethics of its mortuary artist in such debatable matters as the ownership of costly "laying-out" apparel invisible beneath the casket's lid, and the degree of dignity to be maintained in posing and adapting the unseen members of lifeless tenants to containers not always calculated with sublimest accuracy. Most distinctly Birch was lax, insensitive, and professionally undesirable; yet I still think he was not an evil man. He was merely crass of fiber and function – thoughtless, careless, and liquorish, as his easily avoidable accident proves, and without that modicum of imagination which holds the average citizen within certain limits fixed by taste.

Just where to begin Birch's story I can hardly decide, since I am no practiced teller of tales. I suppose one should start in the cold December of 1880, when the ground froze and the cemetery delvers found they could dig no more graves till spring. Fortunately the village was small and the death rate low, so that it was possible to give all of Birch's inanimate charges a temporary haven in the single antiquated receiving tomb. The undertaker grew doubly lethargic in the bitter weather, and seemed to outdo even himself in carelessness. Never did he knock together flimsier and ungainlier caskets, or disregard more flagrantly the needs of the rusty lock on the tomb door which he slammed open and shut with such nonchalant abandon.

At last the spring thaw came, and graves were laboriously prepared for the nine silent harvests of the grim reaper which waited in the tomb. Birch, though dreading the bother of removal and interment, began his task of transference one disagreeable April morning, but ceased before noon because of a heavy rain that seemed to irritate his horse, after having laid but one mortal tenement to its permanent rest. That was Darius Peck, the nonagenarian, whose grave was not far from the tomb. Birch decided that he would begin the next day with little old Matthew Fenner, whose grave was also near by; but actually postponed the matter for three days, not getting to work till Good Friday, the 15th. Being without superstition, he did not heed the day at all; though ever afterward he refused to do anything of importance on that fateful sixth day of the week. Certainly, the events of that evening greatly changed George Birch.

On the afternoon of Friday, April 15th, then, Birch set out for the tomb with horse and wagon to transfer the body of Matthew Fenner. That he was not perfectly sober, he subsequently admitted; though he had not then taken to the wholesale drinking by which he later tried to forget certain things. He was just dizzy and careless enough to annoy his sensitive horse, which as he drew it viciously up at the tomb neighed and pawed and tossed its head, much as on that former occasion when the rain had vexed it. The day was clear, but a high wind had sprung up; and Birch was glad to get to shelter as he unlocked the iron door and entered the side-hill vault. Another might not have relished the damp, odorous chamber with the eight carelessly placed coffins; but Birch in those days was insensitive, and was concerned only in getting the right coffin for the right grave. He had not forgotten the criticism aroused when Hannah Bixby's relatives, wishing to transport her body to the cemetery in the city whither they had moved, found the casket of Judge Capwell beneath her headstone.

The light was dim, but Birch's sight was good, and he did not get Asaph Sawyer's coffin by mistake, although it was very similar. He had, indeed, made that coffin for Matthew Fenner; but had cast it aside at last as too awkward and flimsy, in a fit of curious sentimentality aroused by recalling how kindly and generous the little old man had been to him during his bankruptcy five years before. He gave old Matt the very best his skill could produce, but was thrifty enough to save the rejected specimen, and to use it when Asaph Sawyer died of a malignant fever. Sawyer was not a lovable man, and many stories were told of his almost inhuman vindictiveness and tenacious memory for wrongs real or fancied. To him Birch had felt no compunction in assigning the carelessly made coffin which he now pushed out of the way in his quest for the Fenner casket.

It was just as he had recognized old Matt's coffin that the

door slammed to in the wind, leaving him in a dusk even deeper than before. The narrow transom admitted only the feeblest of rays, and the overhead ventilation funnel virtually none at all; so that he was reduced to a profane fumbling as he made his halting way among the long boxes toward the latch. In this funereal twilight he rattled the rusty handles, pushed at the iron panels, and wondered why the massive portal had grown so suddenly recalcitrant. In this twilight, too, he began to realize the truth and to shout loudly as if his horse outside could do more than neigh an unsympathetic reply. For the long-neglected latch was obviously broken, leaving the careless undertaker trapped in the vault, a victim of his own oversight.

The thing must have happened at about three-thirty in the afternoon. Birch, being by temperament phlegmatic and practical, did not shout long; but proceeded to grope about for some tools which he recalled seeing in a corner of the tomb. It is doubtful whether he was touched at all by the horror and exquisite weirdness of his position, but the bald fact of imprisonment so far from the daily paths of men was enough to exasperate him thoroughly. His day's work was sadly interrupted, and unless chance presently brought some rambler hither, he might have to remain all night or longer. The pile of tools soon reached, and a hammer and chisel selected, Birch returned over the coffins to the door. The air had begun to be exceedingly unwholesome; but to this detail he paid no attention as he toiled, half by feeling, at the heavy and corroded metal of the latch. He would have given much for a lantern or bit of candle; but lacking these, bungled semi-sightlessly as best he might.

When he perceived that the latch was hopelessly unyielding, at least to such meager tools and under such tenebrous conditions as these, Birch glanced about for other possible points of escape. The vault had been dug from a hillside, so that the narrow ventilation funnel in the top ran through several feet of earth, making this direction utterly useless to consider. Over the door, however, the high, slit-like transom in the brick facade gave promise of possible enlargement to a diligent worker; hence upon this his eyes long rested as he racked his brains for means to reach it. There was nothing like a ladder in the tomb, and the coffin niches on the sides and rear – which Birch seldom took the trouble to use – afforded no ascent to the space above the door. Only the coffins themselves remained as potential stepping-stones, and as he considered these he speculated on the best mode of arranging them. Three coffin-heights, he reckoned, would permit him to reach the transom; but he could do better with four. The boxes were fairly even, and could be piled up like blocks; so he began to compute how he might most stably use the eight to rear a scalable platform four deep. As he planned, he could not but wish that the units of his contemplated staircase had been more securely made. Whether he had imagination enough to wish they were empty, is strongly to be doubted.

Finally he decided to lay a base of three parallel with the wall, to place upon this two layers of two each, and upon these a single box to serve as the platform. This arrangement could be ascended with a minimum of awkwardness, and would furnish the desired height. Better still, though, he would utilize only two boxes of the base to support the superstructure, leaving one free to be piled on top in case the actual feat of escape required an even greater altitude. And so the prisoner toiled in the twilight, heaving the unresponsive remnants of mortality with little ceremony as his miniature Tower of Babel rose course by course. Several of the coffins began to split under the stress of handling, and he planned to save the stoutly built casket of little Matthew Fenner for the top, in order that his feet might have as certain a surface as possible. In the semi-gloom he trusted mostly to touch to select the right one, and indeed came upon it almost by accident, since it tumbled into his hands as if through some odd volition after he had unwittingly placed it beside another on the third layer.

The tower at length finished, and his aching arms rested by a pause during which he sat on the bottom step of his grim device, Birch cautiously ascended with his tools and stood abreast of the narrow transom. The borders of the space were entirely of brick, and there seemed little doubt but that he could shortly chisel away enough to allow his body to pass. As his hammer blows began to fall, the horse outside whinnied in a tone which may have been encouraging and may have been mocking. In either case it would have been appropriate; for the unexpected tenacity of the easy-looking brickwork was surely a sardonic commentary on the vanity of mortal hopes, and the source of a task whose performance deserved every possible stimulus.

Dusk fell and found Birch still toiling. He worked largely by feeling now, since newly gathered clouds hid the moon; and though progress was still slow, he felt heartened at the extent of his encroachments on the top and bottom of the aperture. He could, he was sure, get out by midnight – though it is characteristic of him that this thought was untinged with eerie implications. Undisturbed by oppressive reflections on the time, the place, and the company beneath his feet, he philosophically chipped away the stony brickwork; cursing when a fragment hit him in the face, and laughing when one struck the increasingly excited horse that pawed near the cypress tree. In time the hole grew so large that he ventured to try his body in it now and then, shifting about so that the coffins beneath him rocked and creaked. He would not, he found, have to pile another on his platform to make the proper height; for the hole was on exactly the right level to use as soon as its size might permit.

It must have been midnight at least when Birch decided he could get through the transom. Tired and perspiring despite many rests, he descended to the floor and sat a while on the bottom box to gather strength for the final wriggle and leap to the ground outside. The hungry horse was neighing repeatedly and almost uncannily, and he vaguely wished it would stop. He was curiously unelated over his impending escape, and almost dreaded the exertion, for his form had the indolent stoutness of early middle age. As he remounted the splitting coffins he felt his weight very poignantly; especially when, upon reaching the topmost one, he heard that aggravated crackle which bespeaks the wholesale rending of wood. He had, it seems, planned in vain when choosing the stoutest coffin for the platform; for no sooner was his full bulk again upon it than the rotting lid gave way, jouncing him two feet down on a surface which even he did not care to imagine. Maddened by the sound, or by the stench which billowed forth even to the open air, the waiting horse gave a scream that was too frantic for a neigh, and plunged madly off through the night, the wagon rattling crazily behind it.

Birch, in his ghastly situation, was now too low for an easy scramble out of the enlarged transom; but gathered his energies for a determined try. Clutching the edges of the aperture, he sought to pull himself up, when he noticed a queer retardation in the form of an apparent drag on both his ankles. In another moment he knew fear for the first time that night; for struggle as he would, he could not shake clear of the unknown grasp which held his feet in relentless captivity. Horrible pains, as of savage wounds, shot through his calves; and in his mind was a vortex of fright mixed with an unquenchable materialism that suggested splinters, loose nails, or some other attribute of a breaking wooden box. Perhaps he screamed. At any rate he kicked and squirmed frantically and automatically whilst his conscious- ness was almost eclipsed in a half-swoon.

Instinct guided him in his wriggle through the transom, and in the crawl which followed his jarring thud on the damp ground. He could not walk, it appeared, and the emerging moon must have witnessed a horrible sight as he dragged his bleeding ankles toward the cemetery lodge; his fingers clawing the black mold in brainless haste, and his body responding with that maddening slowness from which one suffers when chased by the phantoms of nightmare. There was evidently, however, no pursuer; for he was alone and alive when Armington, the lodge-keeper, answered his feeble clawing at the door.

Armington helped Birch to the outside of a spare bed and

sent his little son Edwin for Dr. Davis. The afflicted man was fully conscious, but would say nothing of any consequence; merely muttering such things as "oh, my ankles!", "let go!", or "shut in the tomb." Then the doctor came with his medicine-case and asked crisp questions, and removed the patient's outer clothing, shoes, and socks. The wounds – for both ankles were frightfully lacerated about the Achilles' tendons – seemed to puzzle the old physician greatly, and finally almost to frighten him. His questioning grew more than medically tense, and his hands shook as he dressed the mangled members; binding them as if he wished to get the wounds out of sight as quickly as possible.

For an impersonal doctor, Davis' ominous and awestruck cross-examination became very strange indeed as he sought to drain from the weakened undertaker every least detail of his horrible experience. He was oddly anxious to know if Birch were sure – absolutely sure – of the identity of that top coffin of the pile; how he had chosen it, how he had been certain of it as the Fenner coffin in the dusk, and how he had distinguished it from the inferior duplicate coffin of vicious Asaph Sawyer. Would the firm Fenner casket have caved in so readily? Davis, an old-time village practitioner, had of course seen both at the respective funerals, as indeed he had attended both Fenner and Sawyer in their last illnesses. He had even wondered, at Sawyer's funeral, how the vindictive farmer had managed to lie straight in a box so closely akin to that of the diminutive Fenner.

After a full two hours Dr. Davis left, urging Birch to insist at all times that his wounds were caused entirely by loose nails and splintering wood. What else, he added, could ever in any case be proved or believed? But it would be well to say as little as could be said, and to let no other doctor treat the wounds. Birch heeded this advice all the rest of his life till he told me his story; and when I saw the scars – ancient and whitened as they then were – I agreed that he was wise in so doing. He always remained lame, for the great tendons had been severed; but I think the greatest lameness was in his soul. His thinking processes, once so phlegmatic and logical, had become ineffaceably scarred; and it was pitiful to note his response to certain chance allusions such as "Friday," "tomb," "coffin," and words of less obvious concatenation. His frightened horse had gone home, but his frightened wits never quite did that. He changed his business, but something always preyed upon him. It may have been just fear, and it may have been fear mixed with a queer belated sort of remorse for bygone crudities. His drinking, of course, only aggravated what it was meant to alleviate.

When Dr. Davis left Birch that night he had taken a lantern and gone to the old receiving tomb. The moon was shining on the scattered brick fragments and marred facade, and the latch of the great door yielded readily to a touch from the outside. Steeled by old ordeals in dissecting rooms, the doctor entered and looked about, stifling the nausea of mind and body that everything in sight and smell induced. He cried aloud once, and a little later gave a gasp that was more terrible than a cry. Then he fled back to the lodge and broke all the rules of his calling by rousing and shaking his patient, and hurling at him a succession of shuddering whispers that seared into the bewildered ears like the hissing of vitriol.

"It was Asaph's coffin, Birch, just as I thought! I knew his teeth, with the front ones missing on the upper jaw – never, for God's sake, shew those wounds! The body was pretty badly gone, but if ever I saw vindictiveness on any face – or former face. . . . You know what a fiend he was for revenge – how he ruined old Raymond thirty years after their boundary suit, and how he stepped on the puppy that snapped at him a year ago last August. . . . He was the devil incarnate, Birch, and I believe his eye-for-an-eye fury could beat old Father Death himself. God, what a rage! I'd hate to have it aimed at me!

"Why did you do it, Birch? He was a scoundrel, and I don't blame you for giving him a cast-aside coffin, but you always did go too damned far! Well enough to skimp on the thing some way, but you knew what a little man old Fenner was.

"I'll never get the picture out of my head as long as I live. You kicked hard, for Asaph's coffin was on the floor. His head was broken in, and everything was tumbled about. I've seen sights before, but there was one thing too much here. An eye for an eye! Great heavens, Birch, but you got what you deserved. The skull turned my stomach, but the other was worse – *those ankles cut neatly off to fit Matt Fenner's cast-aside coffin!*"

THE VERY OLD FOLK

Thursday
[November 3, 1927]

Dear Melmoth:–

. . . So you are busy delving into the shady past of
that insufferable young Asiatic Varius Avitus Bassianus?
Ugh! There are few persons I loathe more than that
cursed little Syrian rat!

I have myself been carried back to Roman times by
my recent perusal of James Rhoades' *Æneid*, a translation never before read by me, and more faithful to
P. Maro than any other versified version I have ever
seen – including that of my late uncle Dr. Clark, which
did not attain publication. This Virgilian diversion,
together with the spectral thoughts incident to All
Hallows' Eve with its Witch-Sabbaths on the hills,
produced in me last Monday night a Roman dream of
such supernal clearness and vividness, and such titanic
adumbrations of hidden horror, that I verily believe I
shall some day employ it in fiction. Roman dreams
were no uncommon features of my youth – I used to
follow the Divine Julius all over Gallia as a Tribunus
Militum o'nights – but I had so long ceased to experience them, that the present one impressed me with
extraordinary force.

It was a flaming sunset or late afternoon in the tiny
provincial town of Pompelo, at the foot of the
Pyrenees in Hispania Citerior. The year must have
been in the late republic, for the province was still
ruled by a senatorial proconsul instead of a prætorian
legate of Augustus, and the day was the first before

the Kalends of November. The hills rose scarlet and
gold to the north of the little town, and the westering
sun shone ruddily and mystically on the crude new
stone and plaster buildings of the dusty forum and
the wooden walls of the circus some distance to the
east. Groups of citizens – broad-browed Roman colonists and coarse-haired Romanized natives, together
with obvious hybrids of the two strains, alike clad in
cheap woolen togas – and sprinklings of helmeted
legionaries and coarse-mantled, black-bearded
tribesmen of the circumambient Vascones – all
thronged the few paved streets and forum; moved by
some vague and ill-defined uneasiness.

I myself had just alighted from a litter, which the
Illyrian bearers seemed to have brought in some haste
from Calagurris, across the Iberus to the southward.
It appeared that I was a provincial quæstor named L.
Cælius Rufus, and that I had been summoned by the
proconsul, P. Scribonius Libo, who had come from
Tarraco some days before. The soldiers were the fifth
cohort of the XIIth legion, under the military tribune
Sex. Asellius; and the legatus of the whole region, Cn.
Balbutius, had also come from Calagurris, where the
permanent station was.

The cause of the conference was a horror that
brooded on the hills. All the townsfolk were frightened, and had begged the presence of a cohort from
Calagurris. It was the Terrible Season of the autumn,
and the wild people in the mountains were preparing
for the frightful ceremonies which only rumor told
of in the towns. They were the very old folk who
dwelt higher up in the hills and spoke a choppy
language which the Vascones could not understand.
One seldom saw them; but a few times a year they
sent down little yellow, squint-eyed messengers (who

looked like Scythians) to trade with the merchants
by means of gestures, and every spring and autumn
they held the infamous rites on the peaks, their howl-
ings and altar-fires throwing terror into the villages.
Always the same – the night before the Kalends of
Maius and the night before the Kalends of November.
Townsfolk would disappear just before these nights,
and would never be heard of again. And there were
whispers that the native shepherds and farmers were
not ill-disposed toward the very old folk – that more
than one thatched hut was vacant before midnight
on the two hideous Sabbaths.

This year the horror was very great, for the people
knew that the wrath of the very old folk was upon
Pompelo. Three months previously five of the little
squint-eyed traders had come down from the hills, and
in a market brawl three of them had been killed. The
remaining two had gone back wordlessly to their
mountains – and this autumn not a single villager had
disappeared. There was menace in this immunity. It
was not like the very old folk to spare their victims
at the Sabbath. It was too good to be normal, and the
villagers were afraid.

For many nights there had been a hollow drumming on the hills, and at last the ædile Tib. Annæus
Stilpo (half native in blood) had sent to Balbutius at
Calagurris for a cohort to stamp out the Sabbath on
the terrible night. Balbutius had carelessly refused,
on the ground that the villagers' fears were empty,
and that the loathsome rites of hill folk were of no
concern to the Roman People unless our own citizens
were menaced. I, however, who seemed to be a close
friend of Balbutius, had disagreed with him; averring
that I had studied deeply in the black forbidden lore,
and that I believed the very old folk capable of visiting

almost any nameless doom upon the town, which after all was a Roman settlement and contained a great number of our citizens. The complaining ædile's own mother Helvia was a pure Roman, the daughter of M. Helvius Cinna, who had come over with Scipio's army. Accordingly I had sent a slave – a nimble little Greek called Antipater – to the proconsul with letters, and Scribonius had heeded my plea and ordered Balbutius to send his fifth cohort, under Asellius, to Pompelo; entering the hills at dusk on the eve of November's Kalends and stamping out whatever nameless orgies he might find – bringing such prisoners as he might take to Tarraco for the next proprætor's court. Balbutius, however, had protested, so that more correspondence had ensued. I had written so much to the proconsul that he had become gravely interested, and had resolved to make a personal inquiry into the horror.

He had at length proceeded to Pompelo with his lictors and attendants; there hearing enough rumors to be greatly impressed and disturbed, and standing firmly by his order for the Sabbath's extirpation. Desirous of conferring with one who had studied the subject, he ordered me to accompany Asellius' cohort – and Balbutius had also come along to press his adverse advice, for he honestly believed that drastic military action would stir up a dangerous sentiment of unrest amongst the Vascones both tribal and settled.

So here we all were in the mystic sunset of the autumn hills – old Scribonius Libo in his toga prætexta, the golden light glancing on his shiny bald head and wrinkled hawk face, Balbutius with his gleaming helmet and breastplate, blue-shaven lips compressed in conscientiously dogged opposition, young Asellius

with his polished greaves and superior sneer, and the
curious throng of townsfolk, legionaries, tribesmen,
peasants, lictors, slaves, and attendants. I myself seemed
to wear a common toga, and to have no especially
distinguishing characteristic. And everywhere horror
brooded. The town and country folk scarcely dared
speak aloud, and the men of Libo's entourage, who
had been there nearly a week, seemed to have caught
something of the nameless dread. Old Scribonius
himself looked very grave, and the sharp voices of us
later comers seemed to hold something of curious
inappropriateness, as in a place of death or the temple
of some mystic god.

We entered the prætorium and held grave converse.
Balbutius pressed his objections, and was sustained by
Asellius, who appeared to hold all the natives in
extreme contempt while at the same time deeming it
inadvisable to excite them. Both soldiers maintained
that we could better afford to antagonize the minority
of colonists and civilized natives by inaction, than to
antagonize a probable majority of tribesmen and
cottagers by stamping out the dread rites.

I, on the other hand, renewed my demand for
action, and offered to accompany the cohort on any
expedition it might undertake. I pointed out that the
barbarous Vascones were at best turbulent and uncertain, so that skirmishes with them were inevitable
sooner or later whichever course we might take; that
they had not in the past proved dangerous adver-
saries to our legions, and that it would ill become
the representatives of the Roman People to suffer
barbarians to interfere with a course which the
justice and prestige of the Republic demanded. That,
on the other hand, the successful administration of
a province depended primarily upon the safety and

good-will of the civilized element in whose hands
the local machinery of commerce and prosperity
reposed, and in whose veins a large mixture of our
own Italian blood coursed. These, though in numbers
they might form a minority, were the stable element
whose constancy might be relied on, and whose
cooperation would most firmly bind the province to
the Imperium of the Senate and the Roman People.
It was at once a duty and an advantage to afford
them the protection due to Roman citizens; even
(and here I shot a sarcastic look at Balbutius and
Asellius) at the expense of a little trouble and activity,
and of a slight interruption of the draft-playing and
cock-fighting at the camp in Calagurris. That the
danger to the town and inhabitants of Pompelo was
a real one, I could not from my studies doubt. I had
read many scrolls out of Syria and Ægyptus, and the
cryptic towns of Etruria, and had talked at length
with the bloodthirsty priest of Diana Aricina in his
temple in the woods bordering Lacus Nemorensis.
There were shocking dooms that might be called
out of the hills on the Sabbaths; dooms which ought
not to exist within the territories of the Roman
People; and to permit orgies of the kind known to
prevail at Sabbaths would be but little in consonance
with the customs of those whose forefathers, A.
Postumius being consul, had executed so many
Roman citizens for the practice of the Bacchanalia
– a matter kept ever in memory by the Senatus
Consultum de Bacchanalibus, graven upon bronze
and set open to every eye. Checked in time, before
the progress of the rites might evoke anything with
which the iron of a Roman pilum might not be able
to deal, the Sabbath would not be too much for the
powers of a single cohort. Only participants need

be apprehended, and the sparing of a great number of mere spectators would considerably lessen the resentment which any of the sympathizing country folk might feel. In short, both principle and policy demanded stern action; and I could not doubt but that Publius Scribonius, bearing in mind the dignity and obligations of the Roman People, would adhere to his plan of despatching the cohort, me accompanying, despite such objections as Balbutius and Asellius – speaking indeed more like provincials than Romans – might see fit to offer and multiply.

The slanting sun was now very low, and the whole hushed town seemed draped in an unreal and malign glamor. Then P. Scribonius the proconsul signified his approval of my words, and stationed me with the cohort in the provisional capacity of a centurio primipilus; Balbutius and Asellius assenting, the former with better grace than the latter. As twilight fell on the wild autumnal slopes, a measured, hideous beating of strange drums floated down from afar in terrible rhythm. Some few of the legionarii shewed timidity, but sharp commands brought them into line, and the whole cohort was soon drawn up on the open plain east of the circus. Libo himself, as well as Balbutius, insisted on accompanying the cohort; but great difficulty was suffered in getting a native guide to point out the paths up the mountain. Finally a young man named Vercellius, the son of pure Roman parents, agreed to take us at least past the foothills. We began to march in the new dusk, with the thin silver sickle of a young moon trembling over the woods on our left. That which disquieted us most was *the fact that the Sabbath was to be held at all.* Reports of the coming cohort must have reached the hills, and even the lack of a final decision could

not make the rumor less alarming – yet there were
the sinister drums as of yore, as if the celebrants had
some peculiar reason to be indifferent whether or
not the forces of the Roman People marched against
them. The sound grew louder as we entered a rising
gap in the hills, steep wooded banks enclosing us
narrowly on either side, and displaying curiously
fantastic tree-trunks in the light of our bobbing
torches. All were afoot save Libo, Balbutius, Asellius,
two or three of the centuriones, and myself, and at
length the way became so steep and narrow that
those who had horses were forced to leave them; a
squad of ten men being left to guard them, though
robber bands were not likely to be abroad on such
a night of terror. Once in a while it seemed as though
we detected a skulking form in the woods nearby,
and after a half-hour's climb the steepness and
narrowness of the way made the advance of so great
a body of men – over 300, all told – exceedingly
cumbrous and difficult. Then with utter and horri-
fying suddenness we heard a frightful sound from
below. It was from the tethered horses – they had
screamed, not neighed, but *screamed*... and there
was no light down there, nor the sound of any human
thing, to shew why they had done so. At the same
moment bonfires blazed out on all the peaks ahead,
so that terror seemed to lurk equally well before and
behind us. Looking for the youth Vercellius, our guide,
we found only a crumpled heap weltering in a pool
of blood. In his hand was a short sword snatched
from the belt of D. Vibulanus, a subcenturio, and on
his face was such a look of terror that the stoutest
veterans turned pale at the sight. He had killed
himself when the horses screamed... he, who had
been born and lived all his life in that region, and

knew what men whispered about the hills. All the torches now began to dim, and the cries of frightened legionaries mingled with the unceasing screams of the tethered horses. The air grew perceptibly colder, more suddenly so than is usual at November's brink, and seemed stirred by terrible undulations which I could not help connecting with the beating of huge wings. The whole cohort now remained at a standstill, and as the torches faded I watched what I thought were fantastic shadows outlined in the sky by the spectral luminosity of the Via Lactea as it flowed through Perseus, Cassiopeia, Cepheus, and Cygnus. Then suddenly all the stars were blotted from the sky – even bright Deneb and Vega ahead, and the lone Altair and Fomalhaut behind us. And as the torches died out altogether, there remained above the stricken and shrieking cohort only the noxious and horrible altar-flames on the towering peaks; hellish and red, and now silhouetting the mad, leaping, and colossal forms of such nameless beasts as had never a Phrygian priest or Campanian grandam whispered of in the wildest of furtive tales. And above the nighted screaming of men and horses that dæmonic drumming rose to louder pitch, whilst an ice-cold wind of shocking sentience and deliberateness swept down from those forbidden heights and coiled about each man separately, till all the cohort was struggling and screaming in the dark, as if acting out the fate of Laocoön and his sons. Only old Scribonius Libo seemed resigned. He uttered words amidst the screaming, and they echo still in my ears. *"Malitia vetus – malitia vetus est … venit … tandem venit . . ."*

And then I waked. It was the most vivid dream in years, drawing upon wells of the subconscious

long untouched and forgotten. Of the fate of that
cohort no record exists, but the town at least was
saved – for encyclopedias tell of the survival of
Pompelo to this day, under the modern Spanish name
of Pompelona. . . .

                    Yrs for Gothick Supremacy–
              C · IVLIVS · VERVS · MAXIMINVS.

THE EVIL CLERGYMAN

I was shewn into the attic chamber by a grave, intelligent-looking man with quiet clothes and an iron-gray beard, who spoke to me in this fashion:

"Yes, *he* lived here – but I don't advise your doing anything. Your curiosity makes you irresponsible. *We* never come here at night, and it's only because of *his* will that we keep it this way. You know what *he* did. That abominable society took charge at last, and we don't know where *he* is buried. There was no way the law or anything else could reach the society.

"I hope you won't stay till after dark. And I beg of you to let that thing on the table – the thing that looks like a match box – alone. We don't know what it is, but we suspect it has something to do with what *he* did. We even avoid looking at it very steadily."

After a time the man left me alone in the attic room. It was very dingy and dusty, and only primitively furnished, but it had a neatness which shewed it was not a slum-denizen's quarters. There were shelves full of theological and classical books, and another bookcase containing treatises on magic – Paracelsus, Albertus Magnus, Trithemius, Hermes Trismegistus, Borellus, and others in strange alphabets whose titles I could not decipher. The furniture was very plain. There was a door, but it led only into a closet. The only egress was the aperture in the floor up to which the crude, steep staircase led. The windows were of bull's-eye pattern, and the black oak beams bespoke unbelievable antiquity. Plainly, this house was of the old world. I seemed to know where I was, but cannot recall what I then knew. Certainly the town was *not* London. My impression is of a small seaport.

The small object on the table fascinated me intensely. I seemed to know what to do with it, for I drew a pocket electric light – or what looked like one – out of my pocket and nervously tested its flashes. The light was not white but violet, and seemed less like true light than like some radio-active bombardment. I recall that I did not regard it as a common flashlight – indeed, I *had* a common flashlight in another pocket.

It was getting dark, and the ancient roofs and chimney-pots outside looked very queer through the bull's-eye window-panes. Finally I summoned up courage and propped the small object up on the table against a book – then turned the rays of the peculiar violet light upon it. The light seemed now to be more like a rain or hail of small violet particles than like a continuous beam. As the particles struck the glassy surface at the center of the strange device, they seemed to produce a crackling noise like the sputtering of a vacuum tube through which sparks are passed. The dark glassy surface displayed a pinkish glow, and a vague white shape seemed to be taking form at its center. Then I noticed that I was not alone in the room – and put the ray-projector back in my pocket.

But the newcomer did not speak – nor did I hear any sound whatever during all the immediately following moments. Everything was shadowy pantomime, as if seen at a vast distance through some intervening haze – although on the other hand the newcomer and all subsequent comers loomed large and close, as if both near and distant, according to some abnormal geometry.

The newcomer was a thin, dark man of medium height attired in the clerical garb of the Anglican church. He was apparently about thirty years old, with a sallow, olive complexion and fairly good features, but an abnormally high forehead. His black hair was well cut and neatly brushed, and he was clean-shaven though blue-chinned with a heavy growth of beard. He wore rimless spectacles with steel bows. His build and lower facial features were like other clergymen I had seen, but he had a vastly higher forehead, and was darker and more intelligent-looking – also more subtly and concealedly *evil*-looking. At the present moment – having just lighted a faint oil lamp – he looked nervous, and before I knew it he was casting all his magical books into a fireplace on the window side of the room (where the wall slanted sharply) which I had not noticed before. The flames devoured the volumes greedily – leaping up in strange colors and emitting indescribably hideous odors as the strangely hieroglyphed leaves and wormy bindings succumbed to the devastating element. All at once I saw there were others in the room – grave-looking men in clerical costume, one of whom wore the bands and knee-breeches of a bishop. Though I could hear nothing, I could see that they were bringing a decision of vast import to the first-comer. They seemed to hate and fear him at the same time, and he seemed to return these sentiments. His face set itself into a grim expression, but I could see his right hand shaking as he tried to grip the back of a chair. The bishop pointed to the empty case and to the fireplace (where the flames had died down amidst a charred, non-committal mass), and seemed filled with a peculiar loathing. The first-comer then gave a wry smile and reached out with his left hand toward the small object on the table. Everyone then seemed frightened. The procession of clerics began filing down the steep stairs through the trap-door in the floor, turning and making menacing gestures as they left. The bishop was last to go.

The first-comer now went to a cupboard on the inner side of the room and extracted a coil of rope. Mounting a chair, he attached one end of the rope to a hook in the great exposed central beam of black oak, and began making a noose with the other end. Realizing he was about to hang himself, I started forward to dissuade or save him. He saw me and ceased his preparations, looking at me with a kind of *triumph* which puzzled and disturbed me. He slowly stepped down from the chair and began gliding toward me with a positively wolfish grin on his dark, thin-lipped face.

I felt somehow in deadly peril, and drew out the peculiar ray-projector as a weapon of defense. Why I thought it could help me, I do not know. I turned it on – full in his face, and saw the sallow features glow first with violet and then with pinkish light. His expression of wolfish exultation began to be crowded aside by a look of profound fear – which did not, however, wholly displace the exultation. He stopped in his tracks – then, flailing his arms wildly in the air, began to stagger backward. I saw he was edging toward the open stair-well in the floor, and tried to shout a warning, but he did not hear me. In another instant he had lurched backward through the opening and was lost to view.

I found difficulty in moving toward the stair-well, but when I did get there I found no crushed body on the floor below. Instead there was a clatter of people coming up with lanterns, for the spell of phantasmal silence had broken, and I once more heard sounds and saw figures as normally tri-dimensional. Something had evidently drawn a crowd to this place. Had there been a noise I had not heard? Presently the two people (simply villagers, apparently) farthest in the lead saw me – and stood paralyzed. One of them shrieked loudly and reverberently:

"Ahrrh! . . . It be 'ee, zur? Again?"

Then they all turned and fled frantically. All, that is, but one. When the crowd was gone I saw the grave-bearded man who had brought me to this place – standing alone with a lantern. He was gazing at me gaspingly and fascinatedly, but did not seem afraid. Then he began to ascend the stairs, and joined me in the attic. He spoke:

"So you *didn't* let it alone! I'm sorry. I know what has happened. It happened once before, but the man got frightened and shot himself. You ought not to have made *him* come back. You know what *he* wants. But you mustn't get frightened like the other man he got. Something very strange and terrible has happened to you, but it didn't get far enough to hurt your mind and personality. If you'll keep cool, and accept the need for making certain radical readjustments in your life, you can keep right on enjoying the world, and the fruits of your scholarship. But you can't live here – and I don't think you'll wish to go back to London. I'd advise America.

"You mustn't try anything more with that – thing. Nothing

can be put back now. It would only make matters worse to do
– or summon – anything. You are not as badly off as you might
be – but you must get out of here at once and stay away. You'd
better thank heaven it didn't go further. . . .

"I'm going to prepare you as bluntly as I can. There's been a
certain change – in your personal appearance. *He* always causes
that. But in a new country you can get used to it. There's a mirror
up at the other end of the room, and I'm going to take you to
it. You'll get a shock – though you will see nothing repulsive."

I was now shaking with a deadly fear, and the bearded man
almost had to hold me up as he walked me across the room to
the mirror, the faint lamp (i.e., that formerly on the table, not
the still fainter lantern he had brought) in his free hand. This is
what I saw in the glass:

A thin, dark man of medium stature attired in the clerical
garb of the Anglican church, apparently about thirty, and with
rimless, steel-bowed glasses glistening beneath a sallow, olive
forehead of abnormal height.

It was the silent first-comer who had burned his books.

For all the rest of my life, in outward form, I was to be that man!

THE BOOK

My memories are very confused. There is even much doubt as to where they begin; for at times I feel appalling vistas of years stretching behind me, while at other times it seems as if the present moment were an isolated point in a gray, formless infinity. I am not even certain how I am communicating this message. While I know I am speaking, I have a vague impression that some strange and perhaps terrible mediation will be needed to bear what I say to the points where I wish to be heard. My identity, too, is bewilderingly cloudy. I seem to have suffered a great shock - perhaps from some utterly monstrous outgrowth of my cycles of unique, incredible experience.

These cycles of experience, of course, all stem from that worm-riddled book. I remember when I found it - in a dimly lighted place near the black, oily river where the mists always swirl. That place was very old, and the ceiling-high shelves full of rotting volumes reached back endlessly through windowless inner rooms and alcoves. There were, besides, great formless heaps of books on the floor and in crude bins; and it was in one of these heaps that I found the thing. I never learned its title, for the early pages were missing; but it fell open toward the end and gave me a glimpse of something which sent my senses reeling.

There was a formula - a sort of list of things to say and do - which I recognized as something black and forbidden; something which I had read of before in furtive paragraphs of mixed abhorrence and fascination penned by those strange ancient delvers into the universe's guarded secrets whose decaying texts I loved to absorb. It was a key - a guide - to certain gateways and transitions of which mystics have dreamed and whispered since the race was young, and which lead to freedoms and discoveries beyond the three dimensions and realms of life and matter that we know. Not for centuries had any man recalled its vital substance or known where to find it, but this book was very old indeed. No printing-press, but the hand of some half-crazed monk, had traced these ominous Latin phrases in uncials of awesome antiquity.

I remember how the old man leered and tittered, and made a curious sign with his hand when I bore it away. He had refused to take pay for it, and only long afterward did I guess why. As I hurried home through those narrow, winding, mist-choked water-front streets I had a frightful impression of being stealthily followed by softly padding feet. The centuried, tottering houses on both sides seemed alive with a fresh and morbid malignity – as if some hitherto closed channel of evil understanding had abruptly been opened. I felt that those walls and overhanging gables of mildewed brick and fungous plaster and timber – with fishy, eye-like, diamond-paned windows that leered – could hardly desist from advancing and crushing me . . . yet I had read only the least fragment of that blasphemous rune before closing the book and bringing it away.

I remember how I read the book at last – white-faced, and locked in the attic room that I had long devoted to strange searchings. The great house was very still, for I had not gone up till after midnight. I think I had a family then – though the details are very uncertain – and I know there were many servants. Just what the year was, I cannot say; for since then I have known many ages and dimensions, and have had all my notions of time dissolved and refashioned. It was by the light of candles that I read – I recall the relentless dripping of the wax – and there were chimes that came every now and then from distant belfries. I seemed to keep track of those chimes with a peculiar intent-ness, as if I feared to hear some very remote, intruding note among them.

Then came the first scratching and fumbling at the dormer window that looked out high above the other roofs of the city. It came as I droned aloud the ninth verse of that primal lay, and I knew amidst my shudders what it meant. For he who passes the gateways always wins a shadow, and never again can he be alone. I had evoked – and the book was indeed all I had suspected. That night I passed the gateway to a vortex of twisted time and vision, and when morning found me in the attic room I saw in the walls and shelves and fittings that which I had never seen before.

Nor could I ever after see the world as I had known it. Mixed with the present scene was always a little of the past and a little of the future, and every once-familiar object loomed alien in the new perspective brought by my widened sight. From then on I walked in a fantastic dream of unknown and half-known shapes; and with each new gateway crossed, the less plainly could I recognize the things of the narrow sphere to which I had so long been bound. What I saw about me none else saw; and I grew doubly silent and aloof lest I be thought mad. Dogs had a fear of me, for they felt the outside shadow which never left my side. But still I read more – in hidden, forgotten books and scrolls to which my new vision led me – and pushed through fresh gateways of space and being and life-patterns toward the core of the unknown cosmos.

I remember the night I made the five concentric circles of fire on the floor, and stood in the innermost one chanting that monstrous litany the messenger from Tartary had brought. The walls melted away, and I was swept by a black wind through gulfs of fathomless gray with the needle-like pinnacles of unknown mountains miles below me. After a while there was utter blackness, and then the light of myriad stars forming strange, alien constellations. Finally I saw a green-litten plain far below me, and discerned on it the twisted towers of a city built in no fashion I had ever known or read of or dreamed of. As I floated closer to that city I saw a great square building of stone in an open space, and felt a hideous fear clutching at me. I screamed and struggled, and after a blankness was again in my attic room, sprawled flat over the five phosphorescent circles on the floor. In that night's wandering there was no more of strangeness than in many a former night's wandering; but there was more of terror because I knew I was closer to those outside gulfs and worlds than I had ever been before. Thereafter I was more cautious with my incantations, for I had no wish to be cut off from my body and from the earth in unknown abysses whence I could never return.

IBID

(". . . as Ibid says in his famous *Lives of the Poets*."
—From a student theme.)

The erroneous idea that Ibid is the author of the *Lives* is so frequently met with, even among those pretending to a degree of culture, that it is worth correcting. It should be a matter of general knowledge that Cf. is responsible for this work. Ibid's masterpiece, on the other hand, was the famous *Op. Cit.* wherein all the significant undercurrents of Graeco-Roman expression were crystallized once for all – and with admirable acuteness, notwithstanding the surprisingly late date at which Ibid wrote. There is a false report – very commonly reproduced in modern books prior to Von Schweinkopf's monumental *Geschichte der Ostrogothen in Italien* – that Ibid was a Romanized Visigoth of Ataulf's horde who settled in Placentia about 410 A.D. The contrary cannot be too strongly emphasized; for Von Schweinkopf, and since his time Littlewit[1] and Bêtenoir,[2] have shewn with irrefutable force that this strikingly isolated figure was a genuine Roman – or at least as genuine a Roman as that degenerate and mongrelized age could produce – of whom one might well say what Gibbon said of Boethius, "that he was the last whom Cato or Tully could have acknowledged for their countryman." He was, like Boethius and nearly all the eminent men of his age, of the great Anician family, and traced his genealogy with much exactitude and self-satisfaction to all the heroes of the republic. His full name – long and pompous according to the custom of an age which had lost the trinomial simplicity of classic Roman nomenclature

---

1 *Rome and Byzantium: A Study in Survival* (Waukesha, 1869), Vol. XX, p. 598.

2 *Influences Romains dans le Moyen Age* (Fond du Lac, 1877), Vol. XV, p. 720.

– is stated by Von Schweinkopf[1] to have been Caius Anicius
Magnus Furius Camillus Æmilianus Cornelius Valerius Pompeius
Julius Ibidus; though Littlewit[2] rejects *Æmilianus* and adds
Claudius Decius Junianus; whilst Bêtenoir[3] differs radically,
giving the full name as Magnus Furius Camillus Aurelius Antoninus
Flavius Anicius Petronius Valentinianus Aegidus Ibidus.

The eminent critic and biographer was born in the year 486,
shortly after the extinction of the Roman rule in Gaul by Clovis.
Rome and Ravenna are rivals for the honor of his birth, though it
is certain that he received his rhetorical and philosophical training
in the schools of Athens – the extent of whose suppression by
Theodosius a century before is grossly exaggerated by the superficial. In 512, under the benign rule of the Ostrogoth Theodoric,
we behold him as a teacher of rhetoric at Rome, and in 516 he
held the consulship together with Pompilius Numantius Bombastes
Marcellinus Deodamnatus. Upon the death of Theodoric in 526,
Ibidus retired from public life to compose his celebrated work
(whose pure Ciceronian style is as remarkable a case of classic
atavism as is the verse of Claudius Claudianus, who flourished a
century before Ibidus); but he was later recalled to scenes of pomp
to act as court rhetorician for Theodatus, nephew of Theodoric.

Upon the usurpation of Vitigcs, Ibidus fell into disgrace and
was for a time imprisoned; but the coming of the Byzantine-
Roman army under Belisarius soon restored him to liberty and
honors. Throughout the siege of Rome he served bravely in the
army of the defenders, and afterward followed the eagles of
Belisarius to Alba, Porto, and Centumcellae. After the Frankish
siege of Milan, Ibidus was chosen to accompany the learned
Bishop Datius to Greece, and resided with him at Corinth in the
year 539. About 541 he removed to Constantinopolis, where he
received every mark of imperial favor both from Justinianus and

---

1   Following Procopius, *Goth.* x.y.z.

2   Following Jornandes, Codex Murat. xxj. 4144.

3   After Pagi, 50–50.

Justinus the Second. The Emperors Tiberius and Maurice did kindly honor to his old age, and contributed much to his immortality – especially Maurice, whose delight it was to trace his ancestry to old Rome notwithstanding his birth at Arabiscus, in Cappadocia. It was Maurice who, in the poet's 101st year, secured the adoption of his work as a textbook in the schools of the empire, an honor which proved a fatal tax on the aged rhetorician's emotions, since he passed away peacefully at his home near the church of St. Sophia on the sixth day before the Kalends of September, A.D. 587, in the 102nd year of his age.

His remains, notwithstanding the troubled state of Italy, were taken to Ravenna for interment; but being interred in the suburb of Classe, were exhumed and ridiculed by the Lombard Duke of Spoleto, who took his skull to King Autharis for use as a wassail-bowl. Ibid's skull was proudly handed down from king to king of the Lombard line. Upon the capture of Pavia by Charlemagne in 774, the skull was seized from the tottering Desiderius and carried in the train of the Frankish conqueror. It was from this vessel, indeed, that Pope Leo administered the royal unction which made of the hero-nomad a Holy Roman Emperor. Charlemagne took Ibid's skull to his capital at Aix, soon afterward presenting it to his Saxon teacher Alcuin, upon whose death in 804 it was sent to Alcuin's kinsfolk in England.

William the Conqueror, finding it in an abbey niche where the pious family of Alcuin had placed it (believing it to be the skull of a saint[1] who had miraculously annihilated the Lombards by his prayers), did reverence to its osseous antiquity; and even the rough soldiers of Cromwell, upon destroying Ballylough Abbey in Ireland in 1650 (it having been secretly transported thither by a devout Papist in 1539, upon Henry VIII's dissolution of the English monasteries), declined to offer violence to a relic so venerable.

---

1   Not till the appearance of Von Schweinkopf's work in 1797 were St. Ibid and the rhetorician properly re-identified.

It was captured by the private soldier Read-'em-and-Weep Hopkins, who not long after traded it to Rest-in-Jehovah Stubbs for a quid of new Virginia weed. Stubbs, upon sending forth his son Zerubbabel to seek his fortune in New England in 1661 (for he thought ill of the Restoration atmosphere for a pious young yeoman), gave him St. Ibid's – or rather Brother Ibid's, for he abhorred all that was Popish – skull as a talisman. Upon landing in Salem Zerubbabel set it up in his cupboard beside the chimney, he having built a modest house near the town pump. However, he had not been wholly unaffected by the Restoration influence; and having become addicted to gaming, lost the skull to one Epenetus Dexter, a visiting freeman of Providence.

It was in the house of Dexter, in the northern part of the town near the present intersection of North Main and Olney Streets, on the occasion of Canonchet's raid of March 30, 1676, during King Philip's War; and the astute sachem, recognizing it at once as a thing of singular venerableness and dignity, sent it as a symbol of alliance to a faction of the Pequots in Connecticut with whom he was negotiating. On April 4 he was captured by the colonists and soon after executed, but the austere head of Ibid continued on its wanderings.

The Pequots, enfeebled by a previous war, could give the now stricken Narragansetts no assistance; and in 1680 a Dutch fur-trader of Albany, Petrus van Schaack, secured the distinguished cranium for the modest sum of two guilders, he having recognized its value from the half-effaced inscription carved in Lombardic minuscules (paleography, it might be explained, was one of the leading accomplishments of New-Netherland fur-traders of the seventeenth century).

Ibiduſ rhetor romanuſ

From van Schaack, sad to say, the relic was stolen in 1683 by a French trader, Jean Grenier, whose Popish zeal recognized the features of one whom he had been taught at his mother's knee to revere as St. Ibide. Grenier, fired with virtuous rage at the possession of this holy symbol by a Protestant, crushed van Schaack's head one night with an axe and escaped to the north with his booty; soon, however, being robbed and slain by the half-breed voyageur Michel Savard, who took the skull – despite the illiteracy which prevented his recognizing it – to add to a collection of similar but more recent material.

Upon his death in 1701 his half-breed son Pierre traded it among other things to some emissaries of the Sacs and Foxes, and it was found outside the chief's tepee a generation later by Charles de Langlade, founder of the trading post at Green Bay, Wisconsin. De Langlade regarded this sacred object with proper veneration and ransomed it at the expense of many glass beads; yet after his time it found itself in many other hands, being traded to settlements at the head of Lake Winnebago, to tribes around Lake Mendota, and finally, early in the nineteenth century, to one Solomon Juneau, a Frenchman, at the new trading post of Milwaukee on the Menominee River and the shore of Lake Michigan.

Later traded to Jacques Caboche, another settler, it was in 1850 lost in a game of chess or poker to a newcomer named Hans Zimmerman; being used by him as a beer-stein until one day, under the spell of its contents, he suffered it to roll from his front stoop to the prairie path before his home – where, falling into the burrow of a prairie-dog, it passed beyond his power of discovery or recovery upon his awaking.

So for generations did the sainted skull of Caius Anicius Magnus Furius Camillus Æmilianus Cornelius Valerius Pompeius Julius Ibidus, consul of Rome, favorite of emperors, and saint of the Romish church, lie hidden beneath the soil of a growing town. At first worshiped with dark rites by the prairie-dogs, who saw in it a deity sent from the upper world, it afterward fell into dire neglect as the race of simple, artless burrowers succumbed before the onslaught of the conquering Aryan. Sewers came, but they passed by it. Houses went up – 2303 of them, and more – and at last one fateful night a titan thing occurred. Subtle Nature, convulsed with a spiritual ecstasy, like the froth of that region's quondam beverage, laid low the lofty and heaved high the humble – and behold! In the roseal dawn the burghers of Milwaukee rose to find a former prairie turned to a highland! Vast and far-reaching was the great upheaval. Subterrene arcana, hidden for years, came at last to the light. For there, full in the rifted roadway, lay bleached and tranquil in bland, saintly, and consular pomp the dome-like skull of Ibid!